FOREVER TEMPTED

ELIZABETH KELLY

EK PUBLISHING INC.

Published by:
EK Publishing Inc.

ISBN: 978-1-77446-042-9

Cover Art by
EK Designs

Author's Note:
This novella is the third book in the Tempted Series.
Please read "Tempted" and "Twice Tempted" **BEFORE** reading this book.

FOREVER TEMPTED

Be tempted one last time.

Life has never been better for Lucy Reid. What started out as an intense and forbidden affair with her boss, Jason, has blossomed into love. Sharing her life with him, loving him, has never been easier. His dominant touch and his desire to possess every part of her brings endless nights of unimaginable pleasure. Their life together is perfect.

But when an earth-shattering revelation threatens their future, Lucy must choose between holding on to what her heart wants most or walking away and allowing Jason the life he deserves.

CHAPTER 1

"Don't be nervous."

"I'm not nervous," Lucy said.

Jason arched his eyebrow at her, and she said, "I'm not nervous – I'm terrified."

He pulled her into his embrace. "You don't need to be. Technically you've already met my parents."

"Video chatting with them a couple of times is not the same as meeting them in person," Lucy said.

He kissed her forehead. "My parents are going to love you."

"Right," Lucy said before squirming out of his embrace. She studied herself in the mirror as Jason pulled on his jeans.

She thought she looked okay for a first parent meeting. Her thick, dark hair was somewhat contained by a clip and she had decided to go with just a bit of blush, a touch of mascara, and some soft pink gloss on her lips. Jason's parents were older, and she didn't want to meet them looking like the whore of Babylon.

Speaking of which – she turned to Jason. "Is my shirt too tight?"

He shook his head as he buckled his belt. "Personally, I don't think it's tight enough."

"Be serious," she said. "Do my boobs look huge?"

He grinned. "Baby, your boobs *are* huge."

"Gah," she muttered. "I really need to look into that reduction surgery."

The look of immediate horror on Jason's face was enough to make her forget her nerves. She laughed as he crossed the room and wrapped his arms around her waist.

"You didn't just say that. Tell me you didn't just say that."

She laughed again. "Careful, honey. Keep acting like that and I'll start to think you're only with me because of my breasts."

He cupped her breasts before kissing her neck. "They're only seventy-five percent of the reason I'm with you."

She whacked him lightly on the ass as he traced the shell of her ear with his tongue. When she spoke, her voice was breathless. "And the other twenty-five percent?"

"Your intelligence and your sweetness," he murmured. He ran his thumb over her nipple and she moaned.

"And the way you look handcuffed to the bed," he continued.

She snorted laughter before nipping his bottom lip. "I'm starting to seriously wonder if you're a sex addict."

He shook his head. "Nope, just a Lucy addict."

"Cheeseball."

He grinned and kissed her, slipping his tongue into her mouth to dart and lick and tease until her hips were pressing against his growing erection.

"I'm not a sex addict," he said before sliding his hand under her shirt.

"I've lived with you for nearly two months, and I can count on one hand the days we haven't had sex," Lucy said.

"We haven't had sex today," Jason said. "Something I fully intend to correct."

"We don't have time," she said as he cupped her breast.

"We have plenty of time." He sucked on the sensitive skin of her throat and she moaned before trying to push away from him.

"We really don't. Your parents' flight arrives in less than two hours and we still have to drive to the airport."

"I'll drive fast." His hands slid behind her back and unclipped her bra before she could even think to stop him.

"Jason," she moaned as he tugged her shirt over her head, stripped away her bra, and latched on to one throbbing nipple. He sucked hard at it as he pushed his hand between her legs and rubbed his thumb roughly against the denim that covered her warmth.

"Dammit, Jason," she muttered as she arched into his hand. "You don't play fair."

He grinned against her breast before pulling on her nipple with his teeth. She cried out and reached for his belt, fumbling the buckle open as he unbuttoned her jeans and shoved them and her panties down her legs.

"We have to be fast," she panted.

"Whatever you want, little Lucy," he replied as he pushed his jeans and briefs down. "Turn around."

She swiveled, resting her hands on the top of the dresser as he bent her over. His hand moved between her thighs again and she spread her legs, pushing her ass into his erection as he thumbed her clit with firm strokes.

He pulled the clip from her hair with his other hand and dropped it to the floor before threading his fingers through the thick, chestnut strands. He pulled hard and she gasped as her head snapped back.

His other hand was still rubbing and pressing against her

3

clit and he growled his approval when wetness coated his fingers. "Fuck, you're so hot, Lucy."

"You too," she panted as she rubbed her pussy shamelessly against his circling fingers. "Fuck me."

"Soon," he promised.

He thrust two fingers into her tight warmth and her entire body shuddered when he rubbed them against her g-spot.

"Oh fuck, oh fuck," she moaned. Her voice was rising, and she hoped that the bedroom window was closed.

"I am going to come if you keep doing that," she warned him.

"We can't have that, now can we?" He kissed her upper back as he withdrew his fingers, and she moaned in dismay.

"Jason, please don't tease me."

He kissed her upper back again. His tongue trailing down her flesh sent shivers up and down her spine, and she grabbed his wrist when he clamped his hand around her full hip.

"Jason, please," she begged loudly. "Fuck me!"

He nudged his knee against her inner thigh. Just the feel of his hair-roughened skin was nearly enough to push her over the edge. She spread her legs further as he pushed up against her. His cock pressed against her entrance and she rose up on her tiptoes as he slid into her with a hard thrust that made her crow loudly in delight.

"Does it feel good, little Lucy?" he panted as he thrust back and forth.

"Yes," she moaned.

He held her steady with one hand around her hip and the other in her hair and plunged back and forth in a steady silken glide that practically liquefied her insides. She moaned loudly and repeatedly as the fluttering in her pelvis and stomach grew to a steady, aching throb.

The blunt head of his cock brushed against her g-spot and

she arched her back, grinding her ass against him as she drew in breath after ragged breath. He leaned over her, she could feel his hot, hurried breath on her damp skin, and kissed her throat before cupping one full breast and squeezing. He fucked her with fast, quick strokes and she met him thrust for thrust as heat pooled in her center.

He pinched her nipple hard, and the bite of pain sent her tumbling over the abyss. She screamed his name, her body shuddering as waves of pleasure washed over her and he made his own hoarse shout before coming deep inside of her.

Her legs were shaking madly, and he held her with one muscled arm around her waist as her breath slowly returned to normal.

"Dammit, we're going to be late. We shouldn't have had sex." Lucy glanced at the alarm clock as Jason pulled out of her.

"I'll try not to take that personally, Luce," he said as he pulled his pants over his hips.

She stuck her tongue out at him as she hurriedly dressed. "Oh God, my hair!"

Her hair had exploded into a giant mass of fuzziness and she snatched her clip from the floor. "C'mon, I'll fix it in the car on the way to the airport."

"You know, Ms. Reid," Jason said as they left the bedroom and walked down the narrow hallway, "it's your fault we're going to be late. If you hadn't looked so delicious in that tight shirt, I wouldn't have felt the need to fuck you."

She stared at him over her shoulder as they walked into the living room. He had a wicked grin on his face, and she stuck her tongue out at him again. "Jason Young, if you don't -"

"Mom? Dad? What are you doing here?" Jason's mouth dropped open, and Lucy snapped her head forward.

Jason's parents, as well as a woman with dark hair and a toned, athletic body, were standing in the living room. The woman was holding Lenny in her arms and she stared at them with an amused grin on her face as Lucy's face flushed a brilliant red.

"Surprise!" Jason's dad said. "We took an earlier flight and decided to grab a cab to your place."

Lucy, her face still the colour of a tomato, watched silently as Jason hurried past her. He hugged his mother and then his father before smiling at the woman holding Lenny. "I didn't know you were going to be here, Carrie."

The woman set Lenny on the floor and hugged Jason. "I had a few days off of work. When Mom and Dad said they were coming to visit, I figured I'd tag along to see my baby brother."

"You should have told me you were catching an earlier flight."

His dad shrugged. "We didn't mind taking a cab. We knocked but there was no answer, so your mother used her key."

His gaze drifted to Lucy standing frozen at the entrance to the living room. "You sounded busy, and we didn't want to interrupt."

Until that moment Lucy hadn't thought it would be possible for her skin to turn any redder. Now she was certain her face was about to burst into flames as Jason's dad grinned at her. Jason was the spitting image of him, and she cursed inwardly when he stared at her hair. She fumbled it into the clip as Jason's mom put her arm around his waist and squeezed.

Oh God, oh God, they heard us. They heard us having sex!

Yeah, they did. Just calm down and take a deep breath. You're an adult for God's sake – act like one!

She took a deep breath and walked toward them, holding her hand out and pasting a smile on her face. "Mr. and Mrs. Young, it's so nice to finally meet you in person."

"It's nice to meet you too, Lucy," Jason's dad replied. The amused grin was still on his face and she forced herself to maintain eye contact as she shook his hand before turning to his mom.

The older woman ignored her outstretched hand and pulled her into her embrace. "We're so happy to meet you!"

Lucy smiled uncertainly at her. "Thank you, Mrs. Young."

"Oh please, call me Rita." Still keeping one thin arm around Lucy's waist, she tugged her toward Jason's sister. "This is Jason's sister, Carrie."

"Hi, Carrie, it's nice to meet you. Jason's told me a lot about you." Lucy held her hand out and Carrie shook it.

"Nice to meet you as well. And don't believe a word he says about me. Except for the part about me beating him up when we were kids. That's completely true."

Lucy smiled nervously as Jason tugged her away from his mother and put his arm around her waist. "Carrie got her black belt in taekwondo when she was seventeen. She practiced most of her moves on me."

"That sounds… nice?" Lucy said and Carrie laughed.

"Well, it did help me move up in belts more quickly."

There was a moment of awkward silence before Jason clapped his father on the back. "C'mon, Dad, I'll help bring in the suitcases from the car."

"So, Mom told me that you and Jason work together?" Carrie said before taking a bite of chicken.

After bringing in the luggage, Jason and Lucy had started lunch. They urged his parents and his sister to sit and relax while Lucy made a salad and Jason barbequed the chicken.

Lucy nodded as Jason passed her the bowl of salad.

"That must be awkward," Carrie said.

"Not really," Jason replied. "I'm not her direct boss and we keep things professional at the office."

He grinned at her and Lucy smiled faintly in reply. That was mostly true. They *had* been keeping things professional since their co-workers discovered their relationship. Of course, none of them had a clue that before they went public with their relationship Jason had spanked her and fucked her over his desk, and she fully intended to keep it that way.

A small shiver went through her and Jason, who was pressed against her thanks to the crowded table, gave her a quizzical look. She squeezed his leg under the table before taking another bite of salad and smiling at Jason's dad.

"How are you enjoying your retirement, Mr. Young?"

"Call me Harvey," he replied. "I'm quite enjoying it, actually. I probably should have retired five years ago but I hate being bored."

"Where are you and Mom traveling first?" Jason asked.

"Actually," Harvey glanced at Rita, "our plans have changed."

Rita grinned at Jason. "We've decided to retire here."

"What? I thought you wanted to travel and see the world," Jason said.

"Well, if your father had retired five years ago, we probably would have." Rita gave Harvey an affectionate look. "We're a little too old to be travelling now and after that pneumonia scare, I want to spend more time with my kids."

"But you'll be moving away from Carrie," Jason said.

"Actually," Carrie cleared her throat, "confession time – I didn't just come down here this weekend to visit you. I'm house hunting as well."

"You're what?" Jason said.

"House hunting. I've been transferred to our office here. I start next month."

Jason stared silently at his family as Rita smiled. "Once we found out Carrie would be moving here, we decided we might as well pack up and join our kids. We've already sold the house and we're looking at a few condominiums tomorrow."

Lucy glanced at Jason. There was a mixture of confusion and happiness skating across his face. She squeezed his leg again before smiling at his parents and sister. "This is wonderful news. I'm so happy Jason will have his family close."

"Do your parents live here?" Rita asked.

Lucy shook her head. "No, they still live in Georgia. I visit them about once a year, and they've been here a few times, but they have busy lives. They're very," a small smile crossed her face, "outgoing and have lots of friends and interests."

"Do you have any siblings?" Carrie asked.

"I don't," Lucy said.

"Why did you move here?" Rita asked.

"A guy, actually," Lucy said. "We broke up about a year later. I thought about moving back home but I'm from a small town and had already fallen in love with the city life. I decided to give it one more year and that was almost four years ago. I'm very glad I decided to stay."

"Me too," Jason squeezed her hand before brushing his lips against her cheek.

"Have your parents met Jason?" Carrie asked.

"Not yet. We're planning a trip in a few months to Georgia," Lucy replied.

"When are you two getting married?" Harvey asked.

Lucy, who had just taken a drink, coughed and choked. Jason patted her on the back.

"Harvey, that's none of our business," Rita said.

"What? He's our kid and this is the first time in a long time that he's looked this happy. They're already living together, why shouldn't they get married?" Harvey said.

He smiled at Lucy as she dabbed at her mouth with a napkin. "You want to marry my kid, right?"

"Dad!" Jason said. "We've been dating for less than four months. Maybe you could cool it with the marriage talk."

Harvey grinned teasingly. "All I'm saying is that we're getting older, and we'd like grandkids before we die."

Carrie laughed. "Could you be any more of a cliché, Dad? Give it a rest, old man."

Harvey winked at her. "Be careful or I'll start hounding you for grandkids."

"In that case – Lucy when are you going to make an honest man out of my baby brother?" Carrie said.

"Oh my God, enough," Jason groaned. "Any more marriage or baby talk and the three of you are sleeping on the deck tonight."

"Jason is right," Rita said. "It's really none of our business." She hesitated before smiling at Lucy. "But before we change the subject - you do want children, don't you, Lucy?"

"Mom!"

Lucy patted Jason's thigh. "Yes, I do want children."

"Oh, thank goodness," Rita said with a sigh of relief.

"How is work going?" Harvey asked Jason and Lucy gave her own inward sigh of relief at the change in subject.

JASON HELPED LUCY PLACE THE BLANKET ON THE FOLD-OUT couch in the den. They'd insisted that his parents take their room and they set Carrie up on the couch in the living room with sheets and blankets. As they climbed into the small and rather lumpy bed, Lenny jumped up and purred before kneading at Lucy's thigh. She winced and pushed him gently to the side as Jason molded his warm, hard body to her back. He cupped her breast and squeezed, and she smacked him on the thigh.

"No way, buddy."

"What?" he asked innocently as his hand trailed feather-light over her round stomach.

"We are not having sex with your parents in the room right next to us," she said. "They've already heard us once, or have you forgotten?"

He chuckled and she shivered at the feel of his warm breath on her bare shoulder. "It's not going to surprise them that we have sex."

"Are you not the least bit embarrassed that they heard us?" she said.

He shrugged. "Nope, not really."

She laughed. "You're shameless."

"I can't help it if you're really sexy." He pressed his growing erection against her ass, and she forced herself not to push back against him.

"Jason, behave," she said. "It was totally humiliating to meet your parents that way."

He kissed her shoulder. "Sorry, little Lucy."

"It's not your fault," she said. "But I can only imagine what they think of me."

"They love you – just like I said they would."

"You don't know that. We barely know each other."

"That's about to change," he said.

She turned to face him and stroked his face. "You must be happy that your family is moving here."

"I am," he admitted. "How do you feel about it?"

"I'm happy," she said truthfully. "I know how close you are to them."

He smiled and kissed her lightly on the mouth. "Thanks, Luce. I promise we won't spend every weekend with them."

He hesitated before saying, "I'm sorry they were so pushy with the marriage and kids thing."

She shrugged. "Honestly, my parents will probably do the same thing to you. Maybe not the kids part – they're remarkably blasé about having grandkids - but I'm pretty certain they'll harass you to put a ring on it."

He laughed and she shushed him before sliding her arm around his waist and burying her face in his neck. He cupped her breast again and teased her nipple with his thumb until it hardened into a tight peak.

"Jason," she said warningly.

"We'll just be very quiet," he whispered before shifting her closer and squeezing her ass through her panties.

Lucy could feel her resolve weakening and Jason picked up on it like a hawk. He pushed her onto her back and pulled her thighs apart before slipping between them. He rocked his cock against her core and kissed her.

"We really have to be quiet," she whispered.

"Quiet as a mouse," he murmured before kissing her neck.

She arched against him and as he tugged her nightgown over her head.

"I love you, Jason."

"I love you too, Lucy."

CHAPTER 2

"So, his entire family will be here in less than a month?" Amanda took a sip of coffee and stared at Lucy over the paper cup.

"Pretty much. His parents put in an offer on a condo this weekend and it was accepted. His sister found a house she liked and put an offer in on it but they're still in the negotiating stage," Lucy said.

It was Monday at lunch. Earlier this morning she had texted her best friend to see if she could meet for a quick coffee. Amanda was a hairstylist and rarely worked Mondays, and she was more than willing to meet Lucy downtown.

"How do you feel about it?" Amanda asked.

"Fine," Lucy said. "Jason is close to his family and I know he's excited that they'll all be living in the same city."

Amanda paused before grinning at her. "They really heard you having sex, huh?"

Lucy blushed. "Yeah, they really did."

"I can think of worse ways to meet your boyfriend's parents," Amanda said.

"Name one."

"I'll get back to you," Amanda said.

Lucy took a sip of her coffee. "Enough about me. I've been a terrible best friend the last little while, I know."

Amanda shrugged. "Hey, you're in a new relationship and up to your ears in handcuffs and whips. I get it."

"No whips," Lucy said with an impish grin.

"Yet," Amanda replied.

"How is Phil?"

"God, I broke up with him like two weeks ago, Luce."

"What?" Lucy stared at her in shock. "Why? And why didn't you tell me?"

"Because it was no big deal. We both knew it was coming and we ended things amicably."

"But why? I thought Phil was perfect for you. I know you'd only been dating for a month or so, but you seemed to really connect."

"Eh, he was a bit too controlling for me. You know I like my freedom."

Lucy studied her carefully for a moment. "Is it that or is it Jamie?"

"Jamie has nothing to do with it."

"Honey, I know you still love Jamie, but he wasn't good for you and he isn't coming back. You can't let what happen with him affect your new relationships. Not every guy is going to do what he did," Lucy said.

"I know," Amanda said before glancing at her cell phone. "Your lunch is over in ten minutes. Come on, I'll walk you to the office.

"Excuse me, Ms. Reid?"

Lucy swung her office chair around and stared blankly at the giant standing in her office doorway.

"Can I help you?" she asked.

"I'm Max Westman – the new accountant in the office?" The man hesitated before ducking into her office and holding out his hand.

She continued to stare at him. There was no way the guy was an accountant. He was unbelievably tall with short blond hair and a slightly darker beard. His shoulders were massive – he filled the entire doorway – and his hands were the size of hams. Accountants were supposed to be thin and nerdy.

"You are Ms. Reid, right?" He craned back to stare at the nameplate outside of her door.

"Yes, sorry! It's nice to meet you. Jerry mentioned you were starting today." She hurried forward and shook his hand.

"I thought it would be best to walk around the office and introduce myself," he said. "Mr. Young was planning on calling a staff meeting to introduce me, but apparently there was some sort of crisis with the server this morning and he and Jerry are holed up in his office."

Two weeks ago, they had upgraded to a new server. It had been crashing on and off since then and she would have to remind Jason later tonight not to take it out on Carlos. As the only IT person in the office, he'd been working around the clock for the last two weeks to try to solve the problems with the new server.

Jason, usually so quick to acknowledge his staff's hard work, didn't have the best attitude toward the poor guy. At one point, Carlos had made it clear he was interested in Lucy. Despite the fact that he was dating their admin person, Penny, for the last five months, his previous crush had automatically landed him a prime spot on Jason's shit list. Lucy sighed inwardly. Jason was a good man - the best man she knew - but he had a jealous streak a mile wide.

"Ms. Reid?"

She smiled apologetically at Max. "I'm sorry, what did you say?"

"I asked what you did for the company."

"I'm a copy editor," Lucy replied. "You know, you look nothing like an accountant."

He laughed. "I get that a lot. Accountants are skinny little guys, right?"

She blushed and his grin widened. "Some of us accountants like to break the mold."

"Well, you certainly have," she laughed. "How tall are you, anyway?"

He hesitated and she said, "I'm sorry, that was rude. You probably get asked that all the time."

"It is a popular question," he said. "I'm 6'7".

"Holy crap," Lucy breathed.

He laughed again. "And that's the popular reaction."

She took a few steps back so she wouldn't have to crane her neck quite so much to meet his gaze. "Have you met everyone yet?"

"Almost. I spent most of the morning going over the notes that the previous accountant left for me – Maureen was her name, I think?"

Lucy nodded and he continued, "Anyway, I decided it was time to take a small break from the exciting world of numbers and meet my coworkers."

"Are you from here?" Lucy asked.

Max shook his head. "No, I moved here for the job. I've been here two weeks and I'm still living out of boxes and trying to remember which one has my frying pan in it. I might be the only single guy I know who would rather cook a meal than go out to eat."

He glanced at his watch. "Anyway, it's almost lunch so I'd better go. You don't happen to know a good sushi place near the office, do you?"

"There's a place over on Third Avenue. It has all-you-can-eat sushi on Thursdays and a bunch of us from the office usually go there once a month. In fact, I think Penny is organizing something for tomorrow. I'll tell her to add you to the invite list."

"Thanks, Ms. Reid." He held his hand out and she shook it again.

"Call me Lucy."

"Lucy."

He smiled and continued to hold her hand. "Say, you wouldn't like to have lunch with me, would you?"

Shit, Lucy thought. His light blue eyes had glided down her body and there was no mistaking the appreciative look in them.

"Oh, that's really nice of you to offer but -"

"Lucy?" Jason stuck his head into her office. "I'm sorry but I need to bail on lunch today. The server has crashed again and -"

He stopped, his eyes narrowing when he saw the way Max held her hand. He walked into her office. Lucy tugged her hand free as Jason stood beside her.

"What are you doing in here, Max?" he asked.

"Just introducing myself to Lucy," Max said.

Jason studied him before turning to Lucy. "I have to cancel our lunch. I'm sorry."

"It's fine," she said. "I'll grab something from the café downstairs. Do you want a sandwich?"

He shook his head. "No, I'll eat later."

"I'll join you at the café, if you don't mind?" Max said.

"Oh, uh," Lucy hesitated, "I was just going to grab a sandwich to eat at my desk so…"

"I'll walk downstairs with you and grab something too," Max said.

"Sure," Lucy said.

She twitched in surprise when Jason put his arm around her and tugged her toward him. He pressed a brief but thorough kiss on her mouth before smiling at her. "I'll see you tonight at home, Lucy."

He squeezed her waist, nodded to Max, and left her office. Lucy cleared her throat. "I'll just grab my purse."

"Sure," Max said.

He followed her out of the office and down the hallway to the elevator. She pushed the button and as they waited for it to arrive, Max said, "So, I guess I don't have to ask if you're single."

She flushed. "Jason and I have been dating for a few months."

"No policy on interoffice dating then?"

"Not really. HR had us sign a document that stated we wouldn't let our personal relationship affect our working one," Lucy said. "We keep things professional at the office."

A small grin crossed Max's face as they entered the elevator. "Yes, it looked professional."

Lucy blushed. "Honestly, he's not normally like that. He's just, uh…"

"The jealous type?" Max asked.

She nodded and he grinned cheerfully at her. "Well, tell Mr. Young he has nothing to worry about. I don't go after women who are in relationships."

"I'll let him know," Lucy laughed.

"Do you get flak from the others for dating the boss?" he asked.

When she didn't reply he said, "Sorry, I'm pretty blunt and nosy – not a great combination."

She laughed again. "Actually, I find it refreshing. And no, surprisingly not. I was worried about it at first – we kept our relationship a secret for a while – but after the initial shock, most people don't seem to care."

"That's good," he replied. "Who else is single in the office?"

"I take it you're not looking to be a bachelor anymore?"

"Is it that obvious?"

"Maybe a little," she teased. "There are a few single ladies in the office. Oh, and Paul is single – if you're also into men?"

"Strictly girls for me, I'm afraid," he said.

"Well, you've got options if you're looking for an office romance."

The elevator doors opened, and they stepped into the lobby. He followed her to the café, ducking to get through the doorway.

"It must be a pain in the ass to be that tall," Lucy said.

He shrugged. "I'm used to it. I was this height by the time I was eighteen. I was skinny as hell though. My nickname was beanpole through most of high school and university. I started to fill out by about twenty-two and I was doing some serious weight-training halfway through university. By the time I graduated, the 'beanpole' nickname was forgotten."

"Do you still do a lot of weight training?" she asked as they joined the line.

"Yeah, my last girlfriend said I was addicted to it, but I like being in good physical shape. Plus, I might be slightly scarred by the beanpole teasing. Does that make me sound less manly?"

She patted his wide forearm. "Not in the least. Childhood teasing can be pretty damaging."

They were at the front of the counter now and she grinned to herself as Max placed his order. He was handsome enough and seemed like a good guy. She wondered how long it would be before Alex was organizing another office bet to see who would bed him first.

"THAT," JASON PUT HIS ARMS AROUND HER WAIST AND KISSED the side of her neck, "smells delicious."

"Thanks." She kissed his cheek before finishing chopping the peppers and added them to the pan to sauté with the rest of the vegetables. "How's it going with the server?"

Jason sat down at the small table, loosening his tie and petting Lenny when the cat jumped into his lap.

"It crashed again at three," he said irritably.

"I know. I left at just after four when it was apparent I wasn't going to be able to access any of my files for the rest of the day. Did Carlos get it up and running again?"

He grimaced as she handed him a bottle of water. "Finally. It took nearly three hours. I'm starting to seriously question the guy's IT credentials."

"Carlos is good at what he does, Jason. Don't let your personal feelings for him influence what you think of his work."

"I'm not," he protested.

She picked up a raw baby carrot, tossing it at him and clapping when he caught it in his mouth. "You are."

"He has a crush on you," Jason muttered around a mouthful of carrot.

"He's been dating Penny for months. His crush is long over," she pointed out before stirring the sizzling vegetables.

"How was your lunch with Max?"

"We didn't have lunch together," she said. "We walked down to the café together and then had lunch in the staff room with everyone else."

"Is he single?"

"Yes."

Jason didn't reply and she turned around to see the familiar look on his face. "He's not interested in me, Jason. I love you but the jealousy thing needs to go down a notch."

The scowl on his face turned into an impish grin. "Hey, can I help it if my girlfriend is so hot that every man who meets her wants to date her?"

She sighed. "I know, right? It's a burden that I bear remarkably well, I think." She slapped her own ass and grinned at him over her shoulder. "You just need to get used to the fact that I'm incredibly attractive but also used to beating away the men with a stick. I don't need you slipping me the tongue in front of my coworkers to keep them at bay."

"There was absolutely no tongue involved in today's kiss. It was a very professional tongue-free kiss. Totally appropriate for the office."

"Yes, well, Max got the message loud and clear so well done," Lucy said. "And get that smug look off of your face."

Jason stood and stripped off his suit jacket, draping it over his arm before kissing her. "You like my smugness."

He slapped her on the ass, and she squealed before giving him a mock scowl. "Spanking in the bedroom only, Mr. Young."

"Whatever you say, Ms. Reid," he said.

CHAPTER 3

Three months later

"Lucy! Over here!"

Lucy waved at Carrie and Rita and weaved past the tables of the busy restaurant. She plopped down in her seat and tucked her purse under her chair before leaning over and kissing Rita on the cheek.

"Hi, Rita."

"Hi, honey. How are you?"

"Good, thanks. How are you?"

"I can't complain – I'm having lunch with my girls, aren't I?"

Lucy smiled at her. It had taken maybe – *maybe* – a month for her to fall in love with Jason's mom. The woman was sweet and kind and had welcomed her into their family with open arms. She liked Harvey as well, he was very similar to Jason in both his looks and manners, but Rita had won her over almost immediately.

"Jason was fine with you giving up part of your Saturday to have lunch with his mom and sister?" Rita asked.

"They see each other every day at work, Mom," Carrie said. "I'm sure it's nice for both of them to have a break from each other."

Lucy smiled hesitantly at her. She liked Carrie but she wasn't so certain that Jason's sister liked her. She was almost positive that Carrie disapproved of their relationship but whether it was because Jason was her superior or just a general dislike for her, Lucy wasn't sure.

It doesn't matter if Carrie approves or doesn't like you. Jason loves you – that's what counts.

Very true and she'd never been one to care what others thought, but she couldn't deny that she wanted Carrie to like her. She supposed it was only natural to want the family of the man she loved to like and accept her.

"He was just heading out for an afternoon of surfing," Lucy said. "He told me to tell you both 'hello'."

"Are you still coming over tomorrow night for dinner?" Rita asked. "Harvey's got a new salmon recipe he's dying to try out on us."

"We'll be there," Lucy promised. "How's work going, Carrie?"

"Oh, fine," Carrie said. "Busy as hell right now – I'm actually heading to the office after lunch."

"I'm sorry to hear that," Lucy said. "I had to work a few hours last weekend, but that's pretty unusual."

Carrie shrugged. "I probably wouldn't mind working on a Saturday if my boyfriend was in the office next to me."

It was just an innocent comment, Lucy told herself. *She didn't mean anything by it – stop reading into everything she says for God's sake.*

"What are you having for lunch?" Rita perused the menu in front of her, banishing the small moment of awkwardness.

"I HAVE A LIFE-ALTERING QUESTION TO ASK, LUCE."

Max dropped into the spare chair in her office and gave her a serious look.

"One sec." Lucy studied the screen in front of her, making a few changes to the document before saving the file and leaning back in her chair. "Hit me."

"Should I ask the lady who wins the 'who fucks Max first' bet going around the office to take me with her to Heaven's Gate Spa, or just keep pretending like I don't know the bet exists?"

"Hmm," Lucy placed her finger on her chin and stared at the ceiling of her office. "Depends on who wins the bet, I suppose. Who has the best chance?"

Max leaned forward. "Well, Eileen brought me a coffee from Starbucks this morning 'just because', so that automatically put her in the top three, but Alex upped the ante by leaning over and flashing me her boobs at lunch."

Lucy burst into laughter. "You do know that Eileen is in a relationship, right?"

Max blinked at her. "She is? Then why the hell is she participating in the bet?"

"Maybe she really was just being nice in bringing you a coffee," Lucy said.

"If that was the case, why did she let her ass brush against my arm when she turned to leave?" Max asked.

Lucy laughed again. "Stay away from Eileen, Max. Her boyfriend is a biker."

"Thanks for the tip. I guess that leaves just Alex."

He grinned at the look on Lucy's face. "I see you like her as much as she likes you. She's the one who started the bet, isn't she?"

"Yes. She started the same bet for Jason when he first arrived."

"What?" Max stared at her with a mock look of hurt. "I'm not the only guy in the office you sicko ladies have plotted to try to bed?"

"Um…sure you are?" Lucy said.

Max laughed and sat back in his chair. "So, is that how your relationship started with Jason? You were determined to win a free trip to a spa?"

"Oh God, no," Lucy said. "I don't participate in the office betting pool. How did you find out about the bet, by the way?"

"I have my ways," Max said. "How's the world of copy editing going?"

"Exciting as always. How's the world of numbers?"

"More titillating than you could ever imagine," Max said.

She grinned at him as he ran a hand through his shaggy blond hair. "Hey, do you know of a good hair stylist?"

"As a matter of fact, I do," Lucy said. "My best friend, Amanda, is a stylist and really good. Want me to text her and set up an appointment for you?"

"Sure. I'm available any night this week," Max said as Jason stepped into her office.

"Hello, Jason."

"Hello, Max. Lucy, can I talk to you privately for a moment?" Jason said.

Max stood and grinned at Lucy. "Text me later, okay?"

Lucy nodded as a scowl crossed Jason's face. He smoothed it out almost immediately as Max clapped him on the back and left the room.

Jason shut the door behind him and stared at Lucy. "What are you -"

He stopped and took a deep breath before smiling at her. "Sorry, none of my business. Have you had a chance to look at the document I sent you?"

"I have. I just want to take one more look through it. Do you need it right away?"

"No, after lunch is fine. Paul's sending you two more documents that are a bit of a rush, though."

"I'll start them right away," she replied.

"Okay, thanks. Still on for lunch?"

"Yep."

"Good."

He hesitated and then opened the door. She hurried across the room and shut the door with a soft thud before wrapping her arms around his broad shoulders and kissing him on the mouth.

He cupped her ass and returned the kiss, darting his tongue into her mouth and sliding it across hers in a sensual caress that made her shudder with desire. She moaned before pulling her head back.

"What was that for?" he said.

"Just a reminder of what you're getting tonight," she said.

He grinned wickedly. "I should warn you that I'm in the mood for restraints tonight."

"Sure," she said sweetly. "I'm perfectly fine with chaining you to the bed, Mr. Young."

He growled and squeezed her ass again before nipping at her bottom lip. "Being cheeky gets you extra spankings, Ms. Reid."

She laughed and rested her forehead on his. "Are you having a good day?"

"Yes, how about you?"

"I am."

"Good. I'd better get back to it."

She caught his hand before he could leave. "I'm texting Max with an appointment for a haircut with Amanda."

A brief look of relief crossed his face before he leaned forward and kissed her again. "I'll see you at lunch, little Lucy."

———

AMANDA GROANED AND PRESSED HER HAND AGAINST HER stomach before continuing to sweep around her station. She had her period and, like always, she had horrible cramps. She glanced at her watch before sighing. She had one more appointment before she could close the salon and go home to a hot bath and a large glass of wine. A rather dismal way to spend her Friday evening, she supposed, but at this moment it sounded positively delightful.

The bell over the door chimed and she forced a smile on her face before turning around. "Hi, be right…"

She trailed off, her mouth dropping open. Ducking to get through the doorway, a giant of a man stepped into the salon. He smiled at her and she closed her mouth with a snap.

"Hi there. I have an appointment with Amanda."

She stared at him blankly as he took a few steps toward her. The smile on his face faltered and he glanced around the salon. "My appointment was at seven thirty. Lucy Reid set it up?"

She continued to stare at him, and he cleared his throat. "Maybe I have the wrong salon?"

Say something, idiot!

"Of course, I'm sorry." She leaned the broom against her

chair and held out her hand. "I'm Amanda. You must be Max."

Her hand was swallowed by his large one and she twitched at the feel of his hard calluses. Lucy had said he was an accountant, but he definitely didn't have the hands of an accountant.

Or the body.

She ignored both her inner voice and her urge to look over his large body again. Christ, he was big. She was 5'7", not exactly a waif-like height for a woman, and she was absolutely dwarfed by him. He smelled delicious and she leaned a little closer, inhaling deeply. She realized with embarrassment that she was still holding his hand and she dropped it hurriedly.

"Sorry, it's been a long day and I'm a little off my game."

"No problem."

His voice was like warm velvet, washing over her and making her forget how much her stomach ached. A new throb began in her pelvis and she took a deep breath.

Get a hold of yourself, Amanda. You are not being turned on by a damn voice and if you are, you seriously need to get laid.

"It's nice to meet you, Max. Follow me to the back and I'll wash your hair."

He followed her to the back of the salon. She wondered if he was checking out her ass in her tight skirt as she pointed to the closest chair. "Have a seat."

He sat down and she tucked a cape around his chest, struggling to fasten it around his thick neck. His neck was roughly the size of her thigh and she gave him a quick look. "Is it too tight?"

He shook his head and she watched with some amuse-

29

ment as he tried to scoot his large body down so he could rest his head in the sink. His legs stretched out almost to the wall.

"Sorry, the chair's a bit small."

He grinned at her with the perfect white teeth of a model and she unconsciously ran her tongue over her crooked eyetooth as he said, "Thanks for trying to make me feel better but I'm perfectly aware that I'm the problem – not the chair."

She smiled, keeping her lips closed to hide her crooked tooth. "You must have fun finding clothes that fit."

"I special order a lot of stuff. Shoes are the real problem."

She glanced down at his plain black loafers, her eyes widening a little at the size of them.

You know what they say, Amanda. Big feet, big –
Shut it!

Clearing her throat, she reached over him and turned the water on. She checked the temperature before using the sprayer to wet his thick, blond hair. She squeezed shampoo into her hand and massaged it into his scalp. He closed his eyes as she rubbed and massaged, and she used the opportunity to study his face. He was tanned with broad cheekbones and a broad nose that should have been too big but fit perfectly on him. Normally she didn't care for beards, but she liked the way his looked. A scar slashed across his left eyebrow and, without thinking about it, she leaned closer to get a better look at it. Her breasts pressed against his wide shoulder and his eyes opened. Their faces were kissing distance apart, and she flushed bright red before snapping her head back.

"Sorry. I was just, um, I mean, I saw your scar and…"

She scrubbed his scalp a little harder as he said, "Bar fight."

"I'm sorry?"

"I got the scar in a bar fight."

"Oh. Really?"

"No, not really. I'm an accountant, we tend to avoid bar fights."

She blushed again and he grinned. "I just say that to improve my street cred. In reality, it was back in university. My then-girlfriend and I decided to celebrate the end of mid-terms with some champagne. I'd never opened a bottle of champagne before but didn't want to appear less than manly in front of her, so I manhandled it open. Unfortunately, I was a little too rough with it and when the cork flew off, it shattered the top of the bottle and I was nicked with a small piece of flying glass."

She glanced at the scar again. "A small piece of glass gave you that big of a scar?"

"Nah, it just nicked me. I got the scar when I saw the drop of blood fall from my face to my hand. I fainted and slammed my face against the corner of the coffee table."

She laughed. "You fainted?"

"Yep. I see even the smallest amount of my own blood and I'm down."

She laughed again. "I'm sorry, it's rude of me to laugh. It's just, you're so big and tough looking."

"I know, right? It's really embarrassing. Promise you won't tell anyone."

"Your secret's safe with me," she said. "So, you had to go to the hospital for stitches?"

"Yes. My girlfriend freaked out when I fainted and called 9-1-1. Of course, my face was covered in blood – you'd be amazed at how much your face bleeds when you smash face-first into a coffee table - so I can't really blame her. She broke up with me about a week later. She swore it wasn't because of the fainting but between you and me – I'm pretty certain she was lying. No one wants to date the guy who faints at the sight of blood. It's probably why I'm still single."

She bit back her sudden urge to tell him she was single too. Mostly because she didn't really know if she was or not. She sighed. She really needed to talk to Lucy about what was happening, but she knew what Lucy would say and she guessed that she really didn't want to hear it. She was being an idiot, she knew she was, but you couldn't help who you fell in love with. Even if he could occasionally be the biggest asshole on the planet.

Occasionally? It's more than occasionally and you know it. Just because he's acting different right now doesn't mean shit. Sooner or later the real –

She shut down her inner voice again, a grimace crossing her face, as Max gave her a curious look. "You okay?"

She nodded and he studied her for a moment longer as her period reminded her of its existence and sent another throbbing cramp through her lower belly. She tried not to wince and must have succeeded because he closed his eyes again and relaxed in the chair. She rinsed his hair before using a towel to blot it dry.

"All done. Sit up for me, please."

He sat straight and she scrubbed the towel over his head again before indicating for him to follow her to her station.

MAX STUDIED AMANDA'S ASS AS SHE LED HIM TO HER SALON chair. The woman was downright gorgeous with her long blonde hair and slender body. When he had opened his eyes and seen her face so close to his, her hazel eyes studying him carefully and her soft breasts pressed against his shoulder, he had damn near gotten an erection. Christ, did she smell good.

Something flowery and light that made him think of warm summer days.

She moved the broom and shook the cape out. "Did you want to take off your suit jacket? If hairs get into the collar, it'll be super itchy."

He unbuttoned his jacket and shrugged out of it, setting it on the chair next to hers. Her low voice did things to his insides, delicious things that brought forth images of silk sheets, naked flesh, and her crying his name.

His dick stirred and his eyes dropped to her chest. She was wearing a plain white t-shirt with a V-neck and he could see just a hint of her cleavage. She wasn't overflowing in the chest department, but they would probably be the perfect handful in his large mitt.

"Uh, have a seat," she said.

He realized he had been caught staring at her tits and he cursed inwardly at his lack of self-control before sitting down. The chair creaked alarmingly but held his weight and she draped the cape over his chest.

"You have a tattoo." Her hands had paused in fastening the cape around his neck and she briefly touched the back of his left shoulder through his white dress shirt.

He nodded. "Another university first."

"But how? If you're afraid of blood, how did you get a tattoo?" she asked.

"I couldn't see the blood so I was fine," he said.

"What is it?" She was leaning down, squinting at the tattoo and the scent of her shampoo drifted to him.

"It's a lion."

"Nice. Any particular reason for getting a lion?" She straightened and finished fastening the cape.

"It's my patronus," he said.

Her hands, which were running through his hair, faltered and she stared at him in the mirror. "Patronus?"

He laughed and she smiled, her lip catching on that delightfully crooked eye-tooth before she ran the tip of her tongue over it. He wanted to run *his* tongue over that tooth, wanted to hear the soft moan she would make when he slid his tongue past it and into the warmth of her mouth.

"Tell the truth, please."

"Honestly, I can't remember why I got the lion tattoo but in my defense, I was super high at the time."

She laughed. "I didn't take you for a weed-smoking hippie."

"Technically I was a brownie-eating hippie," he said.

She laughed again and he curled his hands into fists to stop from reaching out and brushing his fingers across her cheek. God but did her skin look soft.

"So, how much do you want taken off?" Her hands were still threading through his hair and it felt amazing.

"I like it fairly short," he said.

"Sounds good." She smiled at him and reached for the scissors.

"WELL, WHAT DO YOU THINK?" AMANDA STARED A BIT apprehensively at Max.

"I love it." He gave her a broad grin, the corners of his eyes crinkling, and warmth infused her belly.

"Good. You have great hair, by the way."

"Thanks."

She unfastened the cape and shook it out as he stood. She helped him into his suit jacket, resisting the urge to smooth her hands over that impossibly broad back and smiled at him when he followed her to the reception desk. She rang it through the cash register, he gave her a generous tip, and she walked him to the door.

He studied the empty salon. "Are you here all alone?"

She nodded. "You were my last appointment for the day, and I sent our receptionist home earlier."

A small frown crossed his face before he checked his watch. "It's pretty late."

"It's fine. I'm not parked that far away, and it won't take me long to close up."

"I'll wait and walk you to your car." He sat down in the armchair in the waiting area and smiled at her.

"Oh no, you don't have to do that," she said. "I'm sure you want to get home and -"

"I don't mind," he said.

She hesitated before nodding. "Okay, well, thank you."

"You're welcome."

Entirely too conscious of his gaze, she hurried through the closing duties before snagging her jacket from the back room. She took a moment to stare at her reflection in the mirror in the washroom. She looked a bit pale and washed out - her stomach was still cramping like a bitch – and she pinched her cheeks to bring a bit of colour to them before stepping out into the salon.

Max was still sitting patiently in the waiting area and she snagged her purse from under the reception desk. "I'm ready to go."

He stepped into the cool night air and she punched in the alarm code before joining him outside. She locked the door and dropped the keys into her purse. "I'm just parked over there."

He held out his arm and after a moment's hesitation she tucked her hand into the crook of his elbow. It brought warmth and a peculiar feeling of security to walk next to him and she smiled up at him. "Thank you again for waiting. That's very nice of you."

"You're welcome, Amanda."

They were already at her car. For a moment, she wished that she had parked at the far end of the lot as she unlocked the door. "Okay, well, goodnight then."

"Amanda?" His hand caught her arm before she could slide into her car.

"Yes?"

"Would you like to have dinner with me?"

She blinked at his straight forwardness. "Oh, um, I…"

Say yes! Her mind screamed at her.

Shut it! Have you forgotten about Jamie?

Screw Jamie! Better yet – screw Max! Pretty please?

"Amanda?" Max's hand touched her arm.

"I'm sorry, Max. I'd better not."

"Why not?" he asked, then made a face. "Sorry, you don't owe me an explanation for saying no. I just felt like we had a connection."

"We don't. I'm sorry," she said.

A look of disappointment flickered across his face before he smiled at her. "Fair enough. It was nice to meet you, Amanda."

"Nice to meet you too, Max. Thanks again for waiting and walking me to my car."

"You're welcome."

He waited until she had climbed into her car and locked the doors before walking briskly across the parking lot to his own vehicle.

You suck.

She sighed and drove toward home. She had done the

right thing. There was no point in going for dinner with Max when her heart belonged to Jamie.

───────

SHE WAS SOAKING IN THE TUB WHEN HIS TEXT ARRIVED. SHE had brought her cell phone with her solely because of that possibility and, her heart thumping, Amanda scanned his text eagerly.

Hey hottie, what u up to?

Smiling happily, she returned his text.

Soaking in a hot bath. How is New York?

She waited, her smile fading when he didn't text back immediately. God, what was she doing? Jamie was like a drug that she couldn't fucking kick. The man had moved to New York four months ago after dumping her and breaking her heart, but here she was – waiting like a pathetic teenage girl for a text. She should never have –

Her phone dinged and a little rush of happiness flooded through her.

Send me a pic. I wanna see those luscious tits.

She bit indecisively at her bottom lip as he texted her again.

C'mon, baby – I need to see ur tits. I miss them.

She lay back in the tub, angled the phone over her chest and snapped a picture. She studied it carefully, cropping out the bit of her lower face that was visible and adding a filter.

You know, the small part of her that didn't seem to be controlled by her love for Jamie, spoke up, *Max wouldn't ask you for a tit pic to add to his spank bank collection.*

She ignored it and sent the picture. She waited for his response, growing more and more nervous when there was no reply. Being nervous was ridiculous, Jamie had seen her boobs hundreds of times, but she could feel it seeping through her anyway.

After half an hour, the bath water cooling and her unease growing, she texted him.

Jamie? Are you still there?

While she waited for his reply, she climbed out of the tub and dried off her shivering body before finishing the last of her wine and sliding into bed. She stared fixedly at her phone, sighing with relief when the text came.

Sorry, baby. I'm still here. Send me more pics.

Not tonight. Already in bed.

Wish I was there with u. Miss u.

Relief washed over her.

I miss you too. Why don't you call me and we'll chat for a bit?

She waited, holding her cell phone in a tense grip, for his reply. Her eyes widened, the hopeful smile disappearing when the picture arrived. Her hands turned to ice and she bit back her soft moan of dismay.

The picture was a selfie of Jamie. He was in bed with a woman, his mouth sucking obscenely at one large breast as the woman arched her back and smiled into the camera.

U need to come by, baby. Here's a pic of last night to remind u of what ur missing.

Her hands shaking so violently she could barely type, she texted him back.

Wrong number, asshole.

She tossed her phone on the bed as hot tears leaked down her face. Her phone rang and biting back her bitter sobs, she hit the answer button and waited silently.

"Amanda? Baby?"

"You asshole," she said.

"I'm sorry," he said. "Baby, it was an accident and -"

"Fucking another woman was an accident or sending me proof was an accident?" she said.

"Baby, you know it's you that I love," Jamie said. "I just – I was feeling lonely last night and that girl, she took advantage of it. I miss you so much."

She laughed bitterly. "Right. You miss me so much you just had to ask her to come back for another round tonight."

"Your picture got me all revved up, baby. I just needed to release a little tension. She doesn't mean anything to me. Come to New York and I'll show you how much I love you. Please, Amanda. I want a second chance."

"Have you gone insane?" she said. "You honestly think I'm going to hop on a flight to New York after what you just sent me?"

"I told you – she doesn't mean anything to me."

"Oh my God, I am such an idiot. I really thought you had changed, you know that?" Tears were flowing freely now, and she swiped them away angrily. "I thought that you were actually sorry for what you had done and that you wanted to make it work this time."

"I do! Amanda, I swear I do. I just – I have needs, baby. You know I need a lot of sex. Being so far away from you is really difficult," Jamie said.

"Unfucking believable," she said. "You really are the biggest asshole I've ever met."

"I'm an asshole?" Anger was starting to creep into his voice. "Fine, maybe I'm an asshole but at least I'm not a controlling little bitch who can't tell the difference between loving someone and smothering them."

She winced, feeling ridiculously guilty as Jamie continued. "I thought *you* had changed, Amanda. I thought you understood that I'm not the type of guy who's going to sit back and let their woman dictate how they're going to run their life. I only cheated on you because you were so goddamn smothering I couldn't take it anymore. If you had given me some fucking breathing room, just trusted that I would be faithful and stopped being so goddamn clingy, I wouldn't have cheated. You think I'm the one with the problem but you're wrong. You're way more fucked up than I'll ever be, sweetheart. You know why you're nearly thirty and still single? Because you have no fucking idea how to be in a relationship. Expecting a guy to be at your beck and call twenty-four seven is seriously fucked up. You need fucking therapy."

Nausea was rolling through her stomach now. Jamie knew her so well, knew every fear and worry that plagued her, and she hated that he could use it so easily against her.

"Fuck you, Jamie. Don't call me again."

"Fine by me, sweetheart. I don't need you or your fucking neuroses in my life. You're not pretty or smart enough to make it worth my -"

She ended the call, her entire body shaking and her stomach throbbing, before setting her phone carefully on the nightstand. She stared at it for a moment before curling up in her cold bed and sobbing.

CHAPTER 4

Lucy knocked again on the door of Amanda's townhouse. She dug the spare key from the bottom of her purse and was just reaching for the handle when the door swung open.

"Amanda? Oh, honey, you look terrible."

Amanda laughed dully. "Thanks, Luce."

"Do you have the flu?" Lucy stepped into the narrow hallway and pressed her hand against Amanda's forehead.

"No. What are you doing here?" she said.

"I stopped by the salon today and they told me you called in sick. I was worried when you didn't return any of my texts."

"Why did you come by the salon?" Amanda traipsed into the kitchen and Lucy followed her.

"I wanted to have lunch and see what you thought of Max. He had an appointment with you last night, right?"

"Yes," Amanda said. She poured herself a glass of water and took a sip of it as Lucy touched her arm.

"Honey? Tell me what's wrong, please."

Her worry grew when Amanda burst into sobs. "I'm an idiot, Luce. I'm such a fucking idiot."

Lucy hugged her tightly and stroked her soft, blonde hair. "You're not, sweetie. Tell me what happened."

"THIS ISN'T YOUR FAULT." LUCY POURED HOT WATER INTO the mugs before dipping the teabags in them. "Jamie is a dickhead."

Amanda shook her head. "It is my fault, Luce. I'm the one who allowed him back into my life. I'm the one who thought that maybe he had changed. There's – there's something wrong with me. Why do I love someone who treats me like this?"

Lucy set the steaming mug of tea in front of her and sat down. "You can't just turn your love off and on for someone like a faucet."

Amanda stared into her tea. "You think I'm a fool, don't you?"

"No," Lucy said. "I think you're confused and lonely and I think Jamie has an unhealthy hold over you. I understand why you started talking to him again, honestly I do, but he's not good for you, honey."

Amanda laughed bitterly. "That's the understatement of the year."

She hesitated before glancing at Lucy. "He's right, you know. I am controlling and – and smothering in a relationship."

"No, you're not," Lucy said. "Don't let him into your head like that, Amanda. Jamie doesn't understand what an actual relationship is. Wanting to be with him is not smothering him."

"I didn't trust him. I didn't trust that he wouldn't cheat on me and I obsessed over it."

"Only because he gave you reason not to trust him. He cheated on you, Amanda."

"Because I thought he would. Because I didn't trust him enough to just be secure in our relationship and -"

"Amanda!" Lucy said. "Jamie cheated on you because he's a lying scumbag who can't keep his dick in his pants. No other reason. And even if – and I'm not saying you were because you weren't – you were smothering, that doesn't give him a reason to cheat. If he didn't like it, he should have spoken to you about it or ended the relationship. Cheating on you was a cowardly, fucked-up thing to do, and he's lucky he moved away, or I'd be cutting off his disease-riddled dick with a dull knife."

Amanda smiled faintly as Lucy took a sip of tea. "Honey, I know this isn't exactly what you want to hear right now but Jamie isn't the right guy for you. You need someone sweet and kind who likes you exactly the way you are. He was forever trying to change you."

"No, he wasn't," Amanda protested.

"Yes, he was," Lucy said. "You dyed your hair red for him, you started wearing those dreadful cropped tops and short skirts. Remember the time you nearly broke your ankle trying to walk in those ridiculous high heels he insisted you wear?"

"He just wanted me to be sexier and he was right – I do dress like an old lady."

"Oh my God, no you don't!" Lucy said. "Listen, I know you still love him, and I understand, really I do, but if he tries to contact you again, you have to ignore him."

"He's not going to," Amanda said. "He's finished with me."

"If that's true – great," Lucy said. "But Jamie's like a fucking bad penny – he always turns up. Promise me you won't text him or answer his calls if he does try again."

"I promise," Amanda said. It would be an easy promise to keep – Jamie would never talk to her again. Her chest ached at the thought and she berated herself internally for feeling something for the man who treated her so badly.

"Why can't I just forget about him?" she said. "Why do I have to love him?"

Lucy squeezed her hand again. "You just need to find someone else, Amanda. Get back on the dating horse and forget about Jamie."

"I can't be in a relationship with someone else when I'm still in love with Jamie," Amanda said. "It isn't fair to them."

"Who said anything about being in a relationship?" Lucy asked. "Just get out there and have some fun. You don't need anything serious right now. Date a bunch of different guys and enjoy your life, for God's sake. There's plenty of other guys out there who would kill for the chance to sex you up."

"Like Max?" Amanda suddenly said. "I know why you sent him to me, Lucy."

Lucy grinned at her. "I might have had some ulterior motives, I'll admit it. I thought he would be perfect for you. He's funny and good looking and -"

"Giant-sized," Amanda said. "Good God, I've never met anyone as big as him."

"I know, right? He makes Jason look tiny and Jason's 6'3"," Lucy said.

"He asked me out to dinner," Amanda admitted.

"Did he?" Lucy grinned delightedly. "See, I told you – you're a hot commodity, gorgeous."

"I turned him down," Amanda said. "I just kept thinking

about Jamie and how much I love him and so I said no. Maybe I should reconsider that dinner invite."

Lucy hesitated. "Normally I'd say go for it but I'm pretty sure that Max is looking for a committed relationship and you're not ready for that yet, honey."

Amanda sighed. "No, I'm not. In fact, I think I need to swear off men completely for a while."

"Hey, let's not be hasty," Lucy said. "Did you hear me when I said you need to go out and have some fun? There's nothing wrong with some casual sex. In fact, it can be just what a girl needs when she's nursing a broken heart."

"I'm not that kind of girl. You know that. I can't just sleep with someone without feeling something for them. But I suck at relationships."

"No, you don't."

"I do," Amanda insisted. "I'm not so self-absorbed that I can't see a little of the truth of what Jamie said. I can be smothering and controlling and it's why I'm still single."

"Amanda -"

"I don't want to talk about this anymore, okay?" Amanda said. "How's Jason?"

Lucy frowned but let the topic drop. "He's fine. He was just going surfing when I left. Lord, that man loves to surf. We've talked about buying a bigger house together and he said he was fine if it wasn't on the beach, but I don't think that's -"

She stopped as Amanda winced and pressed her hand against her stomach.

"What's wrong? Maybe you do have the flu."

She placed her hand on Amanda's forehead again as Amanda shook her head. "No, it's just my period. It started yesterday morning and it's been a bad one."

She glanced up at Lucy. "Luce, what's wrong?"

"What's today?" Lucy said.

"The fifteenth, why?"

Lucy stared at the ceiling for a moment. "I missed my period this month."

"Oh?" Amanda said.

"And I," Lucy hesitated, counting back in her head, "fuck, I don't think I had it last month either."

"Are you sure?" Amanda asked.

"Not entirely. Maybe I did get it, I can't remember."

"When do you remember for sure having it?"

"Um," Lucy thought again. "When Jason's parents moved here. I remember because we were helping them unload the truck and I had killer cramps."

She stared wide-eyed at Amanda. "That was three months ago. I can't believe I missed my period two months in a row and didn't even realize it. I mean, we've been busy but still…"

"Are you pregnant?" Amanda said.

"No, I'm on the pill," Lucy said.

Amanda shrugged. "Sometimes people get pregnant while they're on the pill."

"That's not true. Is it?" Lucy asked.

"It happens. My cousin was conceived while my aunt was on the pill."

"I'm not pregnant," Lucy said but there was doubt in her voice. "I've had months where I've missed my period before. I'm not always regular."

"Have you missed two months in a row before?" Amanda asked.

"No, but… well, shit. I haven't been nauseous or anything like that."

"Lots of women don't have morning sickness. You need to buy yourself a pregnancy test."

"Yeah, I do." She jumped up and poured the rest of the tea down the sink. "Honey, are you going to be okay? I can stay if you need me to."

Amanda shook her head. "God, no. Get your ass to a drugstore and pick up a test. Text me once you've peed on the stick."

"Right," Lucy said. She bent and kissed Amanda on the cheek. "I'll text you later, honey. I love you."

"Love you too, Luce."

HAULING FOUR BAGS OF GROCERIES, LUCY BUMPED HER WAY into the small beach house. She swept Lenny back from the open doorway with her foot and shut the door with her ass before calling Jason's name. There was no reply and she hurried into the kitchen and set the bags on the table. Her bladder was throbbing, and she figured she had maybe two minutes before she wet her damn pants. She searched through the bags for the pregnancy test, cursing under her breath and crossing her legs when she couldn't find the damn thing.

"Screw it," she muttered to herself. "I'll pee on the stick next time."

She ran to the bathroom before heading to the bedroom. She changed into shorts and a t-shirt, smiling when Lenny jumped on the bed and nudged her with his head.

"Hi, sweetie," she cooed before petting him. "Did you miss your mama?"

He meowed before rolling onto his back.

"No way, buddy. I'm not falling for the old 'rub my tummy, I promise I won't bite you' bit again," Lucy said.

She wandered down the hall toward the kitchen. After she

put the groceries away and hid the pregnancy test, she'd hit the beach and see if she could find Jason. He probably –

She jumped, her hand clutching at her chest when she saw Jason standing in the kitchen. He was wearing just a pair of shorts and she could see droplets of water sliding down his broad back. Two of the grocery bags had already been emptied and her stomach dropped.

"Hey, you're back," she said.

He didn't reply and she took another nervous step into the kitchen. "Jason?"

He turned to face her, the pregnancy test box in his right hand, and stared blankly at her. "I just got back and thought I'd put away the groceries for you."

"That was nice of you," she said.

"I thought you were on the pill," he said.

"I am. But I've missed two periods in a row," she said. "I'm probably not pregnant. I feel exactly the same and I'm pretty certain I haven't forgotten to take my birth control every day, but two missed periods is weird for me so I just thought it might be best to -"

"Go pee on this," Jason said. He hurried forward and shoved the box into her hand.

"I just went pee," she protested as he took her arm and propelled her toward the bathroom.

"What? Why didn't you pee on the stick?" he said.

"Because I really had to pee, and I couldn't find the box and I didn't want to wet my pants in the kitchen. Where are we going now?"

He herded her back into the kitchen and grabbed a bottle of water from the fridge. "Drink this, Luce."

"I'm not thirsty. I had a smoothie on the way home and -"

"Oh my God, woman! Drink the water, please!" Jason said.

He twisted off the cap and she took a few large swallows to satisfy him. They stood in silence for a moment before she said, "So, how was surfing?"

He raked his hand through his hair. "You want to talk about surfing right now?"

He paced back and forth in the kitchen, staring at the tiled floor. Her anxiety grew to defcon level five.

"Jason? I didn't mean for this to happen – I swear. I'm sure it's nothing and I'm just being paranoid. I'm sorry."

"Sorry?" He stopped pacing and stared in surprise at her. "You're sorry you might be pregnant?"

"No," she said. "I'm sorry that I'm freaking you out over what's probably nothing."

"I'm not freaking out," he said.

"You kind of are," she replied.

"Drink some more water."

She drank half the bottle. Her stomach was already sloshing from the smoothie, but she was fairly certain Jason would pour the water down her throat if she didn't drink.

He resumed his pacing. "Do you want kids, Lucy?"

"You know that I do," she said.

"No, I mean – do you want kids with me?" He gave her an oddly nervous look.

"Yes."

A look of relief crossed his face. "I love you, Lucy."

"I love you too."

"Do you have to pee yet?"

She couldn't stop the small giggle. "No, not yet."

"Drink some more water."

She finished the bottle of water and shook her head when Jason yanked another bottle from the fridge. "I can't drink more. Just give it half an hour, okay?"

He frowned before nodding. "Right, okay. What do we do now?"

"I'm going to put away the rest of the groceries. Why don't you have a shower and get rid of the salt and the sand?"

"Okay, right," he said.

He hesitated in the doorway of the kitchen. "Holler at me if you have to pee."

This time she laughed out loud. "I'm not letting you watch me pee on the stick, Jason."

He flushed a little before stomping back into the kitchen and kissing her on the mouth. "I love you."

"I love you too. Go have a shower," she said.

"IT SAYS YOU HAVE TO PEE DIRECTLY ON THE ABSORBENT tip," Jason hollered through the closed bathroom door.

She could hear the rustle of the instruction paper and he tapped on the door. "Luce, did you hear what I said?"

"Yes," she said. "I know how to do this, Jason."

There was silence and then, "Have you done this before?"

"No," she said. "But I know how to read."

"Right. Have you peed yet?"

"Honey, do me a favour and go wait in the bedroom. I can't pee with you right outside the door," she said with a laugh.

She waited until his footsteps had faded before unwrapping the pregnancy test.

"HAS IT BEEN FIVE MINUTES YET?" JASON SAID.

She checked the alarm clock. "It's been two minutes."

When he started to stand, she tugged him back into a sitting position on the bed. "Honey, relax. It's probably going to be negative."

He put his arm around her and hugged her against him. "Yeah, probably. It said in the instructions that morning urine was best. Do you think that will affect the test?"

"I don't know," she said before resting her head on his shoulder.

"Do you want a boy or a girl?"

"It doesn't matter to me. How about you?"

"I don't care either."

He checked the alarm clock and she smiled at him. "You know, I've never seen this side of you before."

"What side?"

"Nervous and twitchy. You're always so calm and in control."

"I'm not nervous. You're nervous," he said.

She laughed and a grin broke out on his face. "Okay, fine. I might be a little nervous. Why aren't you?"

"Because I'm ninety-nine percent sure it's going to be negative," she replied.

"Then why did you buy the test?"

"I don't know. Peace of mind for that one percent, I guess."

"Lucy?" Jason stared at her. "No matter what happens, I love you. You know that right?"

She nodded and kissed him. "Yes, and I love you too."

She checked the clock. "It's been five minutes."

"Okay," he said. "Let's do this."

He followed her to the bathroom, standing in the doorway as she picked up the test. She stared at it and he cleared his throat. "Luce? What does it say?"

She turned around and stared wide-eyed at him.

"Lucy?"

"Jason, I – I'm pregnant," she whispered.

"You're pregnant," he repeated.

"Yes." Her hands shaking, she handed the test to him and he stared at the faint blue line.

"Holy shit. You're pregnant."

"Yeah."

He stared weirdly at her and she said, "Jason? Are you – are you okay?"

"Am I okay?"

"Honey, you're freaking me out a little," she said.

"I – you're pregnant."

"How do you feel about that?" she said.

He tossed the test on the counter and yanked her into her embrace before kissing her fiercely. "You're having my baby."

She gave him a bit of a dazed look. "You're happy, then?"

"Happy? Lucy, I'm fucking ecstatic!" he shouted.

Relief flooded through her and she hugged him. "Oh, thank God."

"I love kids!" he said. "I want kids – I want a whole fucking baseball team of kids!"

She blinked at him. "What? You never told me that."

"I didn't want to freak you out. I've wanted to be a dad for as long as I can remember," he said excitedly. "Oh my God, we need to tell my mom and dad!"

"Whoa, slow down, cowboy," Lucy said. "I need to confirm it with the doctor first."

"Yeah, I guess you're right. Will you call Monday and make an appointment?"

He was grinning like a little boy and she could feel an answering smile on her lips. "Yes."

"This is the best news ever, little Lucy," he said.

"I'm glad you think so." She kissed him and squeaked in surprise when he lifted her and set her on the bathroom counter.

"This calls for a celebration," he said before pulling her shirt over her head.

"What did you have in mind, Mr. Young?" she asked as he unclasped her bra and dropped it to the bathroom floor.

"Fucking, Ms. Reid. Lots and lots of fucking," he rasped.

The sudden desire in his voice brought on a surge of lust and she lifted herself eagerly when he tugged at the waistband of her shorts. He pulled them down her legs, dragging her panties with them, before reaching between her legs and cupping her warmth. He kissed her hard, taking her mouth in that rough and possessive manner she had grown to crave, as he rubbed her clit until she was wet and swollen and throbbing.

She yanked at his shorts, sliding them down over his firm ass as he bent his head and sucked her nipple into a tight bud. She moaned and squeezed his ass before rubbing her pussy against his erection. He slid across her clit in a delicious friction that made her hips arch, and she reached between them and grasped his cock.

"Careful, Ms. Reid. It's almost like you think you're in charge," Jason muttered against her mouth.

His hand caught her wrist and she scowled at him. "I need you right now - fuck me."

His eyes flashed and pleasure shuddered through her when his hand threaded through her hair and pulled. He nipped at her throat, worrying the sensitive skin between his teeth as he cupped her breast with his other hand and tugged on her nipple.

"Are you telling me what to do, Ms. Reid?"

"Jason, I need you."

"Are you?" He tugged on her nipple again and she moaned.

"No, I – I'm making a suggestion."

He laughed huskily, the sound sent shivers of delight down her spine, before lifting her off the counter until she was standing before him. He took her hand and led her down the hall to the bedroom.

She started toward the bed, pouting at him when he stopped her.

"You should know, Ms. Reid, that I was going to fuck you right away, but your *suggestion* has given me a change of heart."

"Jason, please," she whispered. "Don't make me wait."

"You beg so sweetly, little Lucy." He sucked on her bottom lip and she moaned when he slid one hand between her thighs. "You're very wet. I could fuck you easily, couldn't I?"

"Yes," she said. "I want you to."

"I know." He grinned wickedly at her before pressing on her shoulders. "On your knees, little Lucy."

She sank obediently to her knees, moaning when Jason brushed the head of his cock over her mouth. She parted her lips and he groaned as he slid his cock into her mouth. She sucked eagerly, grasping the base of him and stroking him as she licked around the ridge of his cock before suckling on just the head. His hands threaded through her hair and he held her firmly as he slid his cock deeper into her mouth. She sucked and licked until he was moaning and his hips were thrusting wildly. She swirled her tongue around the head in the way she knew drove him crazy, and he cursed under his breath before pulling out of her mouth and hauling her to her feet.

He spun her around and bent her over the bed. She braced her hands on the mattress as he pushed her thighs apart, and she made a sharp cry of need when he thrust his cock deep into her throbbing pussy. His hands wrapped around her upper arms and he lifted her upper body off the bed, holding her firmly as he fucked her with long, tantalizing strokes that set her body on fire with lust.

Heat was pooling in her center and she met each of his thrusts with reckless abandonment. Each pump of his hips brushed his cock against her g-spot, and she writhed and moaned as the sweetest tension built within her. He leaned over her, his hot breath puffing against her soft skin, and licked along her spine. She cried out, her back arching as her orgasm flowed through her and her pussy clamped around his cock. He groaned and pumped in and out of her before coming deep within her pulsating warmth. Her body shaking, she collapsed on the bed, smiling when Jason collapsed next to her and pulled her into his embrace.

He kissed the back of her shoulder and nuzzled her damp skin affectionately as she twisted her head to smile at him.

"You, Ms. Reid, are a fantastic fuck."

She burst into laughter and punched him lightly on the thigh. "You need to work on your post-coital sweet talk, Mr. Young."

He grinned and pressed a kiss on her throat. "I'll keep that in mind."

CHAPTER 5

Lucy sat nervously in the exam room. She had gone two days ago for bloodwork and the doctor's office had called this morning to see if she was available for an appointment this afternoon. There was a soft knock and the tension in her stomach ratcheted up another notch as her doctor entered the room. He smiled at her.

"Good afternoon, Lucy."

"Hi, Dr. Flint. How are you?"

"Good, how are you?"

"Good, thanks. A little anxious."

He sat down on the small stool and tapped on the keyboard of his laptop for a moment before turning to her. "So, I have the results of your bloodwork here."

"And?" Lucy said.

"You're not pregnant."

She stared at him in shock. "I'm not?"

He shook his head and she blinked back the hot tears that were threatening. "But the pregnancy test was positive."

"Well," he said, "a false positive is rare but not impossible."

"Are you sure I'm not pregnant?"

He nodded. "Yes. You're not pregnant."

Now the tears did fall, and she wiped them away as Dr. Flint handed her a tissue. She swabbed at her cheeks and blew her nose as she thought about Jason back at the office. He had a meeting that he'd offered to cancel but she had told him not to bother. Now she wished bitterly that he was here with her. He was so excited about having a baby. A low sob broke from her throat and she drew in a deep, hitching breath before wiping at her eyes again.

"I'm sorry," she said.

Dr. Flint gave her a sympathetic look. "That's okay, Lucy. You were actively trying, I assume?"

She shook her head. "No, but when we thought it had happened we were – well – we were pretty happy and excited about it."

She stared at the floor. "I should have known it wasn't true. I'm really careful about taking my birth control every day."

"Birth control isn't a hundred percent foolproof so it was possible," Dr. Flint said.

"Yeah." She stood. "Thanks for letting me know, Dr. Flint. Have a good afternoon."

"Lucy, wait." Dr. Flint indicated for her to sit back down and she sank into the chair.

"Is there something else?"

"Yes, actually. There were some abnormalities in your bloodwork."

"What do you mean?"

"There was an indication of infection."

"Infection?" Lucy gave him a blank look. "What type of infection?"

"That's what we need to find out. You said you haven't had your period in two months. Is that right?"

"Yes."

"And that's unusual?"

"Well, I'm not super regular, I miss a month here or there but never two months in a row," she replied.

Dr. Flint nodded. "Okay. I'd like to do a complete physical today including a pelvic exam. It's been quite a few years since you've had one."

Lucy flushed. She hated having a yearly pap smear and always found a reason not to go. "Yeah, I guess so."

"Yearly pap smears are very important," Dr. Flint said. He tapped on his keyboard again. "Also, I'd like to send you for a pelvic ultrasound."

"What? Why?" Lucy asked.

"Call it a hunch," he said. "I had my office call the ultrasound clinic and they've had a cancellation for later this afternoon. Can you make the appointment?"

"I – I guess so," Lucy said. "I'll have to check with my boss."

"Why don't you give him a call right now," Dr. Flint suggested. "Then I'll have my receptionist call and confirm the appointment."

"Is it really necessary to do it today?" Lucy asked.

Dr. Flint nodded before standing. "Yes, I think so, Lucy. I'll give you a few moments to call your boss and change into the gown."

He left the room and Lucy, a sense of unease growing in her belly, called Jerry.

"LUCY?" JASON DROPPED HIS LAPTOP BAG ON THE COUCH AS Lenny weaved around his legs, meowing loudly.

"I'm out here," she called from the deck.

She was sitting curled up on the futon and he sat down beside her. It was a warm evening, but she was wearing a bulky sweater and when he took her hand, it was ice cold.

"Lucy? What's wrong? I was in that damn meeting for most of the afternoon and when I was finished, Jerry said you called and asked to take the rest of the day off."

She smiled at him and he touched the moisture on her cheeks. "What's wrong, honey? Why didn't you answer my texts? What did the doctor say?"

"I'm not pregnant," she said.

He sat back and stared numbly at her. "Not pregnant."

"Nope." She burst into loud sobs and he pulled her into his lap, rubbing her back as she tucked her face into his neck. "I'm so sorry, Jason."

"You have nothing to be sorry about, honey. But I don't understand – the test came back positive."

"Dr. Flint says it's rare but occasionally you do get a false-positive on home pregnancy tests."

Her chest was hitching, and she sniffed as Jason kissed her forehead. "Don't cry, honey. It's okay."

"I just – I was really happy about it, you know? I mean, I know we weren't planning it but then when I thought I was, I…"

She burst into sobs again. Feeling helpless, he rubbed her back and rocked her. "I know, honey. I was really happy too."

"I know," she sobbed. "I'm so sorry."

"Stop saying that." He kissed her forehead again. "Honey, it's not your fault."

He sat quietly, rubbing her back and pressing kisses

against her temple, until her crying turned into the occasional watery sigh.

"God, what a mess," she said.

"It isn't," he insisted. "So we thought you were pregnant and you're not. It's okay, little Lucy."

He made her sit up so he could smile at her. "It's probably better timing that you're not. I mean, it would have been great if you were and we would have made it work, but now we have time to find a bigger place. This house is too small for kids."

"I guess," she said. "I'm sorry I didn't answer your texts. I didn't want to tell you that way."

She rested her forehead against his and he kissed her. "It's fine. Did you take the rest of the afternoon off because you were upset?"

She shook her head. "No. My bloodwork showed an infection so Dr. Flint wanted to do a complete physical and pelvic exam, as well as a pelvic ultrasound."

"What?" Jason gave her an alarmed look. "What kind of infection?"

"He didn't know," Lucy said. "He just said he had a hunch about something and that's why he booked me for the ultrasound."

"Do you feel okay?" Jason asked.

"I feel fine," Lucy said.

He was giving her a worried look and she kissed him again. "Honestly, Jason, I feel perfectly fine. I'm sure it's nothing to worry about."

"I'm going with you when you get the results," Jason said. "Make sure you look at my work calendar before you book the appointment, okay?"

She nodded and he drew her back into his arms. They

watched the sun setting over the water before Lucy sighed again. "We should start dinner. It's getting late."

"You sit out here and rest," Jason set her gently on the futon. "I'll make dinner."

She shook her head. "I'll help."

He started to protest and she stopped it with a kiss. "I'm fine, Jason. Stop worrying."

***

"NERVOUS?"

"A little," Lucy admitted.

Jason took her hand as they sat in the exam room. "Don't be. I'm sure everything's fine."

Lucy gave him a pale smile and he squeezed her hand. "We'll find out what's wrong and fix it, okay?"

"Okay," she replied as there was a knock at the door and Dr. Flint entered the room.

"Hi, Lucy."

"Hi, Dr. Flint. This is my boyfriend, Jason Young."

Jason stood and shook his hand before returning to his seat and taking Lucy's hand again. They stared at Dr. Flint as he pulled up Lucy's file on his laptop.

"So, my suspicions were correct, Lucy. You have pelvic inflammatory disease," Dr. Flint said.

"What is that?" Lucy asked.

"It's an infection that spreads from the vagina to the cervix and, when left untreated, can spread to the uterine lining and the fallopian tubes," Dr. Flint said. "It's common in women your age and is usually caused from a sexually transmitted disease."

Lucy's mouth dropped open. "I don't have an STI. I was

tested less than six months ago, and it came back negative. Both of us were."

She glanced at Jason. She was mortified but he just squeezed her hand and smiled reassuringly.

"No, you don't. In the swabs I took from your pelvic exam last week, I tested for a number of STIs and you were negative for all of them," Dr. Flint said.

"Then I don't understand," Lucy said. "How can I have an infection from an STI when I've never had one?"

"You had a ruptured appendix about six years ago, is that right?" Dr. Flint said.

Lucy nodded. "Yes."

"Although rare, PID can also be caused by a bowel infection, a severe case of appendicitis or a ruptured appendix. I believe that's what caused yours."

"She's had this infection for six years?" Jason said.

Dr. Flint nodded and Lucy shook her head. "That's impossible. I've been perfectly healthy. I haven't had any problems other than an occasional missed period."

"One of the bad things about PID is that it often doesn't cause any symptoms," Dr. Flint said. "Sometimes there is abdominal pain and fever, or pain during sex. Other times it's simply irregular menstrual cycles."

"So, what do we do to fix it?" Jason asked.

"Antibiotics will help clear up the infection," Dr. Flint said.

Jason smiled at Lucy. "See, no problem."

Dr. Flint cleared his throat. "There's something else."

Small tendrils of fear wormed their way into Jason's stomach as Lucy said, "What?"

"You've had the infection a long time, Lucy. The ultrasound revealed that the infection spread from your cervix to your uterine lining and to your fallopian tubes. Because it's been left unchecked for so long, there's been a lot of damage in the form of scarring."

"What does that mean?" Lucy asked.

"With the scarring on your fallopian tubes, the likelihood of conceiving is very low."

"How low?" Lucy said.

"It's hard to say for sure," Dr. Flint said. "With the length of time you've had the infection and the amount of scarring on your tubes, the chances of them being blocked are extremely high."

He paused and gave her a sympathetic look. "Best estimate on my part – you have less than a five percent chance of getting pregnant."

———

"LUCY, YOU NEED TO TALK TO ME," JASON SAID.

They had spent the entire ride from the doctor's office to the pharmacy and to home in complete silence. He sat down next to her on the couch and rested his hand on her knee.

"What's there to talk about?" Lucy said dully. "I can't get pregnant, and you want a baseball team of kids."

He winced before shifting closer and putting his arm around her. "Honey, it doesn't matter."

"Don't say that," she said. "We want babies, and I can't have them. It matters."

"You don't know that for sure," he said. "Dr. Flint said there's a five percent chance that -"

"No, he said there's *less* than a five percent chance that I'll get pregnant," Lucy said. She suddenly laughed bitterly. "The odds are not in our favour."

"So, we can't have our own kids. We'll adopt," he said.

"Is that what you really want?" She stared up at him.

He hesitated and tears started to course down her cheeks. "Yeah, that's what I thought."

"Lucy, I love you. I want to be with you and I don't care if that means it's just you and me for the rest of our lives. I mean that. If we never have kids, then we'll -"

"Stop," she said suddenly. "Just, please stop. I can't talk about this right now, Jason."

She stood and he grabbed her hand. "Don't shut me out, Luce."

"I'm not," she said wearily. "I need some time to process it, okay?"

"Okay."

"I'm going to lie down for a bit. I have a headache."

"I'll come with you."

Hurt flowed through him when she said, "I'd like to be alone for a while. Do you mind?"

He shook his head and she smiled at him before heading to the bedroom. He paced back and forth with Lenny trailing behind him, before pulling the small velvet box from the inside pocket of his suit jacket. He opened it and stared fixedly at the diamond ring as it glittered in the light. With a heavy sigh he closed the box and tucked it back into his pocket.

"COME IN!" JASON SNAPPED.

The door to his office opened and Jerry stepped into the room.

"What?" Jason glared at him and then sighed when the older man raised his eyebrows. "Sorry, Jerry. Bad day."

"Bad week is more like it. You made Alex cry and Carlos threatened to quit."

Jason scowled. "They're both too sensitive."

Jerry sat down in the chair across from Jason's desk and crossed one leg over his knee. "Normally I'd agree with you but not this time. You've been a real bear all week. Do you want to talk about what's wrong?"

"No," Jason snarled. He scrubbed his hand through his hair before sighing. "It's a long story but we found out last week that Lucy has less than a five percent chance of getting pregnant."

"Jesus, I'm sorry," Jerry said. "I guess I know why Lucy started crying in my office yesterday. I thought maybe you two were having a fight."

"We'd have to be talking to fight," Jason said. "She's shut me out, Jerry. Every time I try to talk to her about it, she refuses. Says she needs time to process it, but it's been a goddamn week and she still won't talk about it. We – we thought she was pregnant, and I made the mistake of telling her that I wanted lots of kids and now…"

He stared miserably at Jerry. "I want kids – I do – but if it comes down to having kids or having Lucy, I'll choose her every time. But she won't let me tell her that. She won't -"

He stopped and stared down at his desk, clearing his throat as Jerry waited.

"Tell me what to do, Jerry," Jason said. "You've known Lucy for a long time. How do I get her to talk to me about this?"

"I don't know," Jerry said. "It's not like her to refuse to talk or try to solve the issue."

"It isn't just the pregnancy thing. She's hardly talking at all. She's pale and shaky and she's like a damn shell of who she used to be. I don't know what to do," Jason said.

Before Jerry could reply there was a knock on the door

and Penny stuck her head into the office. "Jason? I have those files you wanted to look at."

Jerry stood and squeezed Jason's shoulder. "Stop by my office later if you need to talk, okay?"

Jason nodded. "Thanks, Jerry."

———

"MAYBE WE SHOULD CANCEL TONIGHT," JASON SAID.

Lucy shook her head. "We're almost to your parents' place."

He reached across the car and took her hand. "We can have dinner with them another time. Why don't we just turn around and go home? I'll call them and make up an excuse."

"No, it's fine."

"We can order in and sit on the deck and talk."

"I don't want to talk about it," Lucy said irritably. "I've told you I need some time."

"Honey -"

"Please, Jason. Not tonight."

"We need to talk about it eventually," he said.

"I know!" She winced and squeezed his hand. "I'm sorry."

"It's okay."

They drove in silence to his parents' house. As he parked in their driveway, he gave her a worried look.

She sighed. "Stop looking at me like that. Your parents will think something's wrong."

"Something is wrong, Lucy," he said.

She pulled her hand free and opened the car door. He shut the engine off and, his stomach in knots, followed her up the driveway.

"WELL, IT'S ONLY A PART TIME JOB AT THE FABRIC PLACE, but I'm so excited," Rita said. "It'll be nice to get out of the house, even for a few hours, every week."

"I'm trying not to take it personally," Harvey said with a grin as he passed the potatoes to Carrie. "Have some more, hon."

Carrie scooped some potatoes onto her plate and handed the bowl to Jason.

"How's work going for the two of you?" she asked.

"Fine. Busy," Jason said.

"Lucy, have some more to eat," Rita urged. "You're looking a bit pale."

"I'm stuffed but thank you, Rita," Lucy said.

Jason glanced quickly at her. If he didn't know her so well, he would almost believe that there was nothing wrong. She was cheerful and chatty the moment they stepped into his parents' house, but even her carefully applied makeup couldn't completely hide the paleness of her skin or the dark circles under her eyes.

"Jason, honey, do you remember the Mayer family?" Rita asked.

Jason nodded. "I played football with their oldest kid. Dan, I think his name was?"

"Yes, that's right. Well, Dan and his wife just had twin boys. They already have a boy and a girl under the age of five. Can you believe it? They're going to be run off their feet. Four kids!"

"That's why I told your mother only two for us. Never let them outnumber you, you know?" Harvey said with a grin.

Jason smiled faintly as Lucy stared at her plate. Carrie

was giving them a careful, considering look and he scowled at her.

"What?"

"Nothing. What's up with you?" she said.

"Nothing," he muttered.

"Bill and Janine were quite thrilled about it," Rita said. "With Dan's kids and Jody's two boys, that makes six grand-children in total for them."

"Speaking of which," Harvey leaned forward and winked at Jason. "When are you going to make an honest woman out of Lucy and give us some grandchildren?"

"Don't, Dad!" Jason said as Lucy flinched beside him. Her hands were clasped so tightly in her lap that her knuckles were white, and her face had completely lost what little colour it had.

"What?" Harvey was oblivious to the sudden tension that radiated from them. "A guy can't ask when he's going to be a grandpa? We're not getting any younger and I know how badly you want kids."

"Dad, stop," Jason said.

Harvey stared at him in confusion before turning to Lucy. "Did you know that Jason coached our local little league team when he was in high school? He had homework and his own friends to occupy his time, but he was adamant about coaching the kids. He was damn good at it too. The little ones loved him. If you guys have a boy, you'll have to -"

A strangled sob tearing from her throat, Lucy stood so abruptly that her chair fell over. She flinched at the sound and the sorrow in her gaze when she glanced at him made Jason's heart ache for her. Tears were catching in her lashes and she blinked rapidly.

"I'm sorry. I'm suddenly not feeling very well. Jason, could you drive me home?"

He stood and took her hand as his parents and sister stared at them.

"Mom, thanks for dinner. I'll, uh, I'll call you later."

"Lucy, stop!"

Lucy sighed and stopped in the middle of the small living room. "I want to go to bed, Jason."

"No," he said. "I'm sorry, honey, I know you're hurting but we can't avoid this any longer. You need to talk about it."

She kept her back turned to him and he cursed with frustration. "Say something, Lucy."

She turned and he took a step back at the look of anger on her face.

"Say what?" she shouted. "That I've spent every hour, every *minute*, of the last week thinking about how I've ruined your life?"

"What are you talking about?" he shouted back. "You haven't ruined my goddamn life, Lucy!"

"Yes, I have!" she cried. "You want kids, and I can't give them to you."

"Honey, we have other options," he said. "We can look into adoption."

"Adoption," she said bitterly. "Do you have any idea how long that will take, Jason? Even if we get approved, we're looking at years before we can adopt a baby. Not to mention how expensive it is, the hoops we'll have to jump through to do it. I researched it this week and -"

Her voice cut out and she swallowed thickly, "There's no guarantee that we can even adopt."

"It doesn't matter," he said.

"Stop saying that!" she shouted again. "It *does* matter, Jason. It's the only thing that matters."

"It isn't. Lucy, I love you. I want to spend the rest of my life with you whether we have kids or not. It doesn't matter to me that you can't have kids. I want to be with you."

"You're just saying that to try to make me feel better," she said dully.

He strode forward and grabbed her shoulders, shaking her gently. "I'm not. I love you, Lucy, and I know you love me."

"You're right. I do love you, Jason. More than anything. It's why I need to give you the chance to live the life you deserve, the life you want."

"I want a life with you," he said.

She touched his face, her fingers moving delicately across his stubble. "I need to go."

Terror knifed through his heart. "What? Go where?"

"I'll stay with Amanda for a while," she said.

"No!" he shouted. "Lucy, you can't run away from this. You can't run away from us."

She cupped his face and kissed him on the mouth. "I love you, Jason."

He watched dumbly as she left the living room. She returned five minutes later, a small suitcase in her hand, and he started toward her.

"Please don't, Jason. Don't make this harder than it already is."

His shoulders slumped and in a hoarse voice said, "I'm not giving up on us, Lucy."

"Maybe you should."

CHAPTER 6

Lucy studied herself in the mirror. Her face was pale, her eyes puffy, and her hair was completely out of control. She scooped it up into a ponytail before pulling out her compact and powdering her face.

Her skirt was too loose. For the first time in her life, she had lost her appetite completely. In the last two weeks, she probably wouldn't have eaten at all if Amanda hadn't forced her to eat. She blinked back the hot tears that were always so close to the surface now. Fuck, had she ever cried this much in her life? She was surprised she wasn't in the hospital with dehydration.

Every night she stared sleeplessly at the ceiling, replaying the day's events in her head. For the first few days, Jason had tried to speak to her at work, tried to force her to listen, but she had shut him out completely. Eventually he had stopped and kept their conversations strictly work related. It hurt terribly to see him every day but the thought of finding another job terrified her. It was bad enough to not be with Jason, to not hear his warm laugh or feel his arms around her. If she couldn't see him every day, it would kill her.

You're being selfish, Lucy. You walked out on him, but you force him to see you every day just because you're too pathetic to completely give him up. You want him to have the life he deserves but you can't let him go. You're such an asshole.

Tears slipped down her cheeks and she wiped at them savagely as the door opened and Penny stepped into the bathroom.

"Lucy? You okay?" she asked.

"Yes, I'm fine. How are you?"

Penny stood next to her. "Better than you. Have you and Jason really broken up? I mean, I just can't believe it. You two are perfect together."

"I really don't want to talk about it," Lucy said.

"Right, of course. I'm sorry," Penny said. "But you know I'm here if you do, right?"

Lucy nodded before grabbing her purse and hurrying out of the bathroom. She headed to her office, keeping her head down, but she staggered to a stop outside of Jason's office door when she heard Alex's laugh. She stared into his office and jealousy surged through her. Alex was standing next to Jason while he peered at his computer. Lucy had to stop the urge to stomp into the room and punch Alex in the face when she let her hand rest against Jason's broad back.

He's not yours anymore, remember? You broke his heart again. Just walk away.

Her pulse thudding and her stomach rolling with nausea, she hurried to her own office as Alex's low and throaty laugh echoed in her ears.

"WHAT ARE YOU STILL DOING HERE, LUCE? IT'S AFTER seven." Max wandered into her office.

"Just had a few things that needed to be done by tomorrow," she lied. Alex was staying late tonight, as was Jason, and the thought of the two of them alone in the office was killing her. Not when Alex had made it so perfectly clear she was willing to help Jason forget about her.

Jason wouldn't do that to you. You know he wouldn't.

No, he wouldn't, but he was also hurting and sometimes people did stupid things when they were vulnerable.

"Is Alex still here?" she said.

He shrugged. "I have no idea. Why?"

"No reason. Why are you here?"

"Financial statements are due to Jason tomorrow and the way he's been lately – it's probably not a good idea to piss him off with late statements."

Guilt flooded through her and she gave him an uneasy smile. "I'm sorry."

"It's not your fault."

"It is," she blurted out before staring at the floor.

"You okay?" Max asked.

Anger poured into her and it was a welcome relief from the despair. She embraced it and jumped to her feet, glaring at Max. "I'm fine. Why does everyone keep asking me that? Jesus, it's no one's business anyway."

"You're right, I'm sorry," Max said. "But maybe we keep asking because it's obvious that you're not fine."

Her anger deflated like a balloon and, to her absolute horror, she burst into tears at the look of sympathy in Max's eyes. He hesitated before hugging her. She wrapped her arms around his waist and sobbed into his suit jacket as he patted her back.

"Hey there, don't cry. It'll work out."

"It won't," she sobbed. "I hurt him so badly and now he hates me."

"Whatever you said or did can be fixed," Max said.

"It can't be fixed," she sobbed again. "It can't ever be fixed and it's all my fault."

"Don't say that," Max rumbled above her. "Jason loves you and you love him. You can make it work."

"Love isn't enough this time, Max." She mumbled into his jacket. Her flood of tears was beginning to ebb. She leaned back, staring mortified at the smears of makeup on his jacket. "Oh God, I've ruined your jacket."

He shook his head. "Nah, dry cleaning will take it right out."

"I'll pay for it," she offered as she wiped her face.

"Don't worry about it." He was still holding her, and he put his finger under her chin and tipped her face up to his. "Why don't I take you for a drink tonight?

She hesitated and he smiled ruefully at the look on her face. "Friendship gesture only, Luce. Seriously. I'm not trying to hit on you or take advantage of you. I'm a good listener and I think it would do you some good to talk tonight."

She was sorely tempted to do just that but confiding in Max about her and Jason's problem felt wrong. She might consider Max a friend, but Jason didn't, and he wouldn't want the accountant at the office knowing his personal business.

"Thanks, but I think I'm just going to go home," she said.

"You sure?" he asked. "I promise I won't -"

"Get your fucking hands off of her."

Lucy instinctively pushed away from Max as they both turned. Jason stood in the doorway of her office with his hands fisted. She stared at him in alarm as he stepped toward them.

"Easy, man. I was just being her friend," Max said.

"She's mine," Jason snarled at him. "If you touch her again, I'll break your fucking hands."

"Is that so?" Max's voice was mild enough, but his big body had stiffened. Alarm bells blared in Lucy's head.

"Jason, it's all right," she said. "Max and I are only friends. You know that."

"I know that he's touching what's mine," Jason said without taking his eyes from Max's face. "And if he does it again, he'll regret it. Get out of here, Max."

There was a long moment of tense silent before Max glanced at Lucy. "Do you want me to walk you to your car?"

Jason stalked toward them. "You fucking asshole."

Lucy stepped hurriedly between them, holding her hand out to Jason and shaking her head. "Stop, Jason. I mean it."

He stopped, his hot gaze flickering to hers before latching onto Max again.

Lucy smiled at Max. "Thank you, but no. It's best if you go."

"Are you sure?" Max said. "He's pretty pissed off."

"You think I would fucking hurt her?" Jason shouted.

"Jason! Don't!" Lucy said. "I'm fine, Max. Please, just go. I'll see you tomorrow."

Max walked toward the door. Lucy groaned when he paused next to Jason and said, "Just so you know, most women don't like the 'this is my woman, hear me roar' caveman behavior. It's not the fucking Ice Age, dude."

Lucy grabbed Jason's arm, holding him in place, as Max, whistling softly under his breath, strolled out of her office. She dropped her hand and gave Jason a strained smile.

"What the hell was that, Lucy?" he snapped.

"It was nothing. Max is a friend, nothing more."

"It didn't look like he was just being a friend!"

"Oh for God's sake, there is nothing going on between Max and me, Jason. You know that."

"Do I?" he said. "We haven't spoken for two weeks. For all I know you could have moved on by now."

"Moved on?" She stared at him in exasperation. "You think it's that easy for me?"

"It was easy enough for you to walk away from me," he said. "You run away like a scared little mouse the first time we have an issue that can't be easily solved, and then expect me to accept it and fucking move on with my life like you have."

"I haven't moved on!" she shouted.

"You're hugging Max in your goddamn office!" he shouted. "You think I don't know he wants to fuck you?"

"He doesn't. Besides, you're one to talk. I saw Alex in your office earlier today – laughing and touching you. Did she offer to blow you right there in your office or invite you back to her place for the blowjob?"

His mouth gaped open. "Lucy, have you gone insane? You know I don't want Alex. You left me, remember? I'm still in love with you and will be for the rest of my fucking life!"

Guilt stabbed through her and she grabbed her purse and nearly ran for the door. "I have to go."

She twitched when he darted in front of her and slammed the door shut before turning her and pushing her back against it. He knocked her purse to the floor and pressed his large body against hers. Lust lit her up immediately despite her anger as glared at her.

"Do you still love me?" he demanded.

"Of course, I do. Jason I -"

He cut her off with a hard kiss, his mouth slanting across

hers and his tongue stabbing into her mouth. She moaned, her entire body arching against him as he grabbed her wrists and pinned her hands above her head.

He devoured her mouth, biting and licking and sucking on her lips until her head was spinning and every breath of air was sucked from her lungs. She gasped for breath, moaning again, when he dipped his head and bit the base of her neck.

He dropped one hand to the front of her shirt and yanked. Buttons popped off, scattering to the floor as he shoved her bra up and dipped his head. He sucked greedily at her left nipple as his hand squeezed and caressed her right and she cried his name.

She had missed this. Missed his hard body, missed the way he took control and didn't allow her to think or protest or need anything but the feel of his mouth and hands on her body. She struggled against the hand holding her wrists. She needed to sink her hands into his hair, claw her nails across his back, but he growled under his breath and tightened his grip. An even more powerful bite of lust swept through her at being restrained. No one would ever know how to touch her, how to make her feel as alive as Jason did.

He moved his mouth to her ear, sucking on her lobe before muttering, "I'm going to release you. Keep your hands exactly where they are, Lucy, or I'll turn you around and spank you until that fucking delicious ass of yours is covered in my handprints. Do you understand?"

She moaned and nodded, and he nipped her earlobe before releasing her wrists. He removed his jacket and shirt with hard, angry movements, dropping them to the ground as she stared hungrily at his naked chest. She kept her arms up despite her almost undeniable temptation to lower them. She wanted Jason to spank her, missed his spankings with an intensity that both shocked and embarrassed her. As her hands wavered, Jason gave her a hard grin.

"I almost think you want me to spank you, little Lucy. Is that what you want? Do you want to be bent over my lap with your ass in the air and your tight little pussy drenching my thigh? Tell me you want me to spank you and I will."

Her already-damp panties soaked through at his hotly worded command. She moaned helplessly as he shoved her thighs open and reached under her skirt. He gave her another hard and glittering grin before curling his hand around her panties and ripping them away. He stuffed them into his pocket and then sucked her nipple again as his hands unbuckled and unbuttoned his pants and he pulled his cock out.

She stared hungrily at it, licking her lips and wondering if he would force her to her knees and suck him. Her pussy throbbed at the thought.

"Have you missed my cock, Lucy?"

"Yes," she said hoarsely.

"I've missed your wet pussy," he muttered against her mouth before kissing her.

Dimly she was aware of his hands pushing her skirt up around her waist, of the cool wood against her naked ass and the hotter touch of Jason's hands as he cupped her ass and lifted her.

"Tell me what you want," he demanded.

She moaned as his cock brushed back and forth over the wet lips of her pussy. "I want you to fuck me."

He pressed her hard against the door, supporting her with his lower body as he reached between them and guided his cock to her entrance. The head breached her, and she moaned low in her throat when he stopped.

"You're mine, Lucy Reid," he whispered against her throat. "Say it."

"Yours," she said. "Yours, Jason. Always."

He thrust into her and she cried out with pleasure, not caring if there was anyone left in the office to hear her. He reached up and grasped her wrists again, pinning her against the door as he fucked her. She pumped her hips against his, sparks lighting up her nervous system as he ground his pelvis against her.

"Oh God, oh God," she moaned repeatedly as a primal ache started in her belly.

He deftly stroked her to a fevered pitch until she was tense and breathing so raggedly she thought she might pass out. Her vision shimmered and blurred as Jason buried himself in her body. He plunged and retreated, stretching her with deep upward strokes as her greedy body took every inch of him.

He kissed her again, claiming her mouth with a possessive roughness that brought her over the edge. She screamed into his mouth, her body shuddering and her velvet core clamping around him rhythmically as she came. He groaned, his body tensing before he thrust himself deep within her and orgasmed.

"Mine," he whispered as he lowered her to the floor. Her legs were shaking and when she started to collapse, he eased her to the floor of her office and curled his large body around hers. They lay in blissful silence as her heart slowed from its frantic thumping to a normal rhythm. His hand cupped her breast and he kissed the back of her neck as she closed her eyes.

After a few moments, he squeezed her breast and kissed her neck again. "Lucy?"

"Yeah?"

"Do you want to stop at Amanda's and pick up your clothes first or just go home?"

Her body tensed and she sat up, hurriedly adjusting her clothing. Her shirt was ruined, there was no way she could use it to cover herself up. Jason handed her his shirt. "Wear this. I've got an extra one in my office."

"Thanks."

He helped her to her feet, and they finished dressing in silence. Jason caught her hand and squeezed it. "You didn't answer, Luce. Do you want to stop at Amanda's first?"

"Jason," she swallowed thickly, trying not to cry, as he gave her an uncertain look. "What just happened – it doesn't change anything."

"Doesn't it?"

She shook her head. "No. I still – still can't give you what you want."

He sighed harshly and dropped her hand. "I want you. I've told you that."

"No, you want me and you want a family. I can't give that to you."

"I'm getting really tired of you not believing me, of not trusting me to know what exactly it is that I want," he said bitterly.

"I'm sorry," she said. "I – I shouldn't have let this happen tonight. It wasn't fair of me and I apologize. It was a mistake to…"

Anger blazed in his eyes. "So, now fucking me is nothing but a mistake to you?"

"No, that isn't what I meant," she said. "I just – I've given you the wrong idea because I'm weak and I miss you."

"I miss you too. So, come back home," he said.

"I can't. I'm sorry."

"Yeah, you keep saying that."

"Jason, I -"

"No," he said, "I can't keep having this same conversation with you. I can't keep trying to convince you that I love you and want to be with you no matter what. It's driving me insane that you won't believe me and I'm tired of it."

Her bottom lip trembling, she nodded and grabbed her purse. "Okay. I'm sorry for what happened tonight, Jason. I'll stay away from you, I promise."

Tomorrow she would start looking for a new job. The thought of never seeing him again sent panic and adrenaline pumping through her veins but seeing the torment on his face was a thousand times worse. She couldn't keep doing this to him.

She headed for the door, flinching when Jason wrapped his hand around her arm. "Wait for me and I'll walk you to your car."

She shook her head. "You're angry and upset and I'm not going to force you to be around me any longer than necessary. I'll be fine."

"If you think I'm letting you walk to the parking garage on your own, you're insane, Lucy. You were hurt before because I forced you to work late, and I swore I'd never let that happen again."

"That wasn't your fault," Lucy said. "You can't possibly still think it was."

"Just wait for me," he repeated impatiently as he scooped his jacket from the floor and stalked to the door.

LUCY STEPPED QUIETLY INTO AMANDA'S TOWNHOUSE. SHE closed the door, wincing at the loud click, before slipping off her shoes and walking gingerly toward the stairs. She could hear Amanda in the kitchen and as much as she loved her best friend, she didn't want to talk. Her throat was aching, and her stomach was reeling, and she wanted to climb into bed and have yet another pathetic sob fest.

The bottom stair creaked, and she sighed when Amanda called, "Luce? Is that you?"

"Yeah," she climbed another step. "It's been a long day, I'm going to -"

"Come into the kitchen. I made fresh cookies!" Amanda shouted.

"I'm really tired, Amanda. Can I take a raincheck?"

"Nope," Amanda yelled. "Get your cute ass in here, Lucy."

She sighed and dropped her purse on the ground before trudging to the brightly lit kitchen. Amanda was just pulling a tray of cookies from the oven.

"Full disclosure," she said as she set them on the top of the stove and turned off the oven, "these are supposed to be health cookies. They're chocked full of nuts and oats and..."

She stopped and stared at Lucy. "Holy hell, woman. What is going on with your hair?"

Lucy touched her hair self-consciously. Her suspicion that she had just-been-fucked hair was confirmed when Amanda said, "Honey, I'm your best friend and I love you so I'm going to be honest. Wearing your hair in the style of 'I've just been screwed five ways to Sunday' is not the best look for the office. It doesn't exactly scream professional unless you're going for the professional hooker look."

Lucy burst into sudden tears and Amanda gave her a

horrified look before running over and hugging her. "Oh, honey, I'm sorry. I didn't mean to hurt your feelings."

"It's not you," Lucy sobbed. "My hair is like this because Jason and I had sex in my office tonight."

Amanda guided her to a kitchen chair and sat down beside her. "Well, that's a good thing, isn't it? You love him and miss him and it's only natural that -"

"He thought it meant we were back together," Lucy said. "The look on his face when I said it hadn't changed anything – oh, God, Amanda. I'm an idiot."

She buried her face in her hands and sobbed as Amanda rubbed her back. After a few moments, a tissue was pressed into her hand and she wiped at her face and blew her nose before smiling at Amanda. "I'm sorry."

"Lucy," Amanda took her by the shoulders. "I love you, but you *are* a fucking idiot."

Her mouth dropped open, and she stared wide-eyed at Amanda. "I – what?"

Amanda sighed deeply. "You're miserable, Luce. You're sitting here in my kitchen crying your eyes out when we both know you should be at home with Jason."

"Do you want me to leave? Is that what you're saying?" Lucy said as hurt flooded through her.

"Of course I'm not," Amanda said. "You're welcome to stay with me for as long as you need. But, as your best friend, it's my duty to tell you when you're being an idiot. And you're being an idiot."

"This isn't what I need to hear tonight," Lucy mumbled. She started to stand and glared at Amanda when the woman pushed her back into the chair.

"Too fucking bad, because you're gonna hear it," Amanda announced. "It's intervention time, Lucy. I'm no psychiatrist but I've watched multiple marathons of *Intervention* so I'm qualified."

Lucy smiled despite her irritation and Amanda grinned at her before sobering. "You're throwing away your happiness and a chance at something real with Jason. He's a good man, Lucy, and he loves you. Don't throw it away."

"I can't give him what he wants."

"So, you and Jason want kids and you can't have them. Boo-fucking-hoo," Amanda said. "Get the fuck over it. Jason has told you repeatedly that he doesn't care, and you need to believe him. You can adopt and," she held up her hand when Lucy started to protest "yeah, I know it won't be easy but whoever said life was easy? Or fair? If it was, I'd be sitting on some goddamn beach with a man who wanted me and loved me just the way I am. Instead, I'm in love with a fucking serial cheater who treats me like garbage. I spend my weekends watching Bridget *fucking* Jones and binge eating popcorn. You have a man who loves you unconditionally. Stop taking that for granted."

"And in three or five or ten years, when Jason leaves me for someone who will give him kids, what then, Amanda? Isn't it better to end it now then torture myself daily wondering when he'll finally realize that I'm not what he wants after all?" Lucy said.

She gasped when Amanda slapped her briskly across the cheek. "Snap out of it, Lucy!"

"What the hell, Amanda?" Lucy cupped her cheek and glared at her.

"Sorry. I watched *Moonstruck* again last night on Netflix," Amanda said.

"Stop watching that movie!"

"Jason isn't going to leave you, Lucy. Jesus, the way that man looks at you? I've never seen anything like it – unless it's the way you look at him. Fuck, the two of you are sickeningly in love. It makes me want to barf up my popcorn some days, I swear to God."

"You suck at interventions," Lucy said.

"It's my first one. I'll be better the next time," Amanda said.

"I am not doing another intervention with you," Lucy said. "You'll probably waterboard me at the next one."

"I might, if you don't start using that giant brain of yours," Amanda said.

"Well, thanks for the pep talk and the slapping but I'm tired and I -"

"Lucy," Amanda grabbed her hands and squeezed them. "Listen to me, really listen to me – you have a good man who loves you and you need to hold on to that as tightly as you can. Take it from me - that kind of love is worth fighting for."

Lucy stared into Amanda's eyes. They were radiating love and compassion and the tears started to flow down her cheeks again.

"I know," she whispered. "But I'm so afraid of disappointing him, of losing him."

"You're going to lose him if you keep going down this road." Amanda Lucy's tears away briskly. "Okay, I'm done."

She stood and plucked two cookies from the tray before handing one to Lucy. "Here, have a cookie."

"This was the worst intervention ever," Lucy said as she bit into the cookie.

"Are you kidding me? You got slapped around a bit and a cookie. More like it's the *best* intervention ever," Amanda said.

They sat in silence for a moment, chewing at the cookies before Lucy glanced at her. "Hey, Amanda?"

"Yeah?"

"These cookies are awful."

"I know, right?" Amanda stood and spit her mouthful of cookie into the garbage before going to the pantry and retrieving a box of Oreos. She opened them and passed a cookie to Lucy. "I love you, Lucy. You know that, don't you?"

"Yeah, thanks, honey. I love you too."

CHAPTER 7

"Lucy?" Carol's voice buzzed over the intercom and Lucy closed the employment website she was perusing with a guilty click before clearing her throat and picking up the phone.

"Hi, Carol. What's up?"

"I have a Carrie Young here to see you. Can I send her back to your office?"

"Carrie Young is here to see me?" Lucy repeated. "Are you sure?"

"Yes," Carol said with a hint of impatience. Lucy could hear the faint ringing of the other lines in her ear. "Can I send her back?"

"Um, sure. Okay."

She hung up the phone and stood before pacing nervously. Why was Carrie here to see her? She rubbed at her forehead. She had slept terribly, and her head was throbbing. Despite Amanda's intervention last night, she was still uncertain and torn. Everything Amanda said had made sense, but she couldn't get passed the nagging feeling that Jason would eventually leave her. It was stupid but –

"Lucy?"

Carrie was standing in her doorway and Lucy plastered a smile on her face. "Carrie, come on in."

Carrie shut the door behind her and cleared her throat. "I'm sorry to bother you at work."

"It's no bother," she said. "Come sit down."

Carrie sat down and Lucy gave her an uncertain look. "Jason isn't here right now. I think he's gone all afternoon."

"I'm here to see you, not Jason," Carrie said.

"Oh." Lucy didn't know what else to say so she simply sat in her office chair and stared at Jason's sister.

Looking extremely nervous, Carrie picked a piece of lint from her pants. "I know this really isn't any of my business, but I wanted to talk to you about you and Jason."

"Carrie, I don't think -"

"Please," Carrie said. "Just give me five minutes of your time, okay?"

Lucy nodded and Carrie blew her breath out in a harsh rush. "I don't know what happened between you and my brother, he won't say a word to me or our parents about it, but I know he is absolutely miserable without you. We've never seen him like this and frankly, we're worried for him."

Lucy gave her a guilty look and Carrie sighed again. "I know I haven't been the," she paused, "warmest to you and I hope to God that doesn't have anything to do with why you and Jason broke up."

"It doesn't," Lucy said. "You not liking me has nothing to do with it, I promise."

Carrie frowned at her. "I do like you, Lucy. I think you're lovely and perfect for my brother."

Lucy blinked in surprise. "No, you don't."

"I do," Carrie insisted. She hesitated before plunging

forward. "I'm going to tell you something that neither Jason nor my parents know. Can I trust you to keep it to yourself?"

"Yes."

"I didn't move here because I transferred jobs. Well, I did, but I didn't transfer jobs because I was bored like I said."

"Why did you then?" Lucy asked.

"I was sleeping with my boss."

Lucy's mouth dropped open, and Carrie nodded. "Yeah. In my case, it was a stupid thing to do. My company doesn't have a clear policy against coworkers sleeping together either, but it was frowned on by upper management. Eventually our coworkers found out we were sleeping together and," she hesitated, "it caused some issues."

"I'm sorry," Lucy said.

"We were both treated differently almost immediately. I should have found another job, but I was so damn stubborn. Why should either of us quit jobs that we loved just because other people were so judgmental? You know? At the time it seemed the right thing to do. Stand up to them and show that it didn't matter what they said about us or what they whispered behind our backs. He didn't give me preferential treatment because we were sleeping together. In fact, if anything, it made him a bit harder on me. We both had something to prove I guess," she said.

She stared at the floor for a moment before glancing at Lucy. "I loved him – hell, I still do - and he loved me. But the pressure of working together day in and day out, along with the attitude of the people we worked with, eventually tore us apart. We couldn't stop fighting and we lost sight of what was really important. I was going to quit my job, but it was too late. We had said and done too many hurtful things and we could never return to what we were. So, when the transfer came up, I took it and I walked away from him."

"You regret it," Lucy said.

"Every damn day," Carrie replied.

She sniffed and Lucy handed her a tissue. Carrie dabbed at her eyes before smiling at Lucy. "I don't know if it's the work thing that's causing this, but I wanted – *needed* – to tell you that it isn't worth it. If you love Jason as much as I suspect you do, then don't make the same mistake that I did."

Lucy blinked back her own tears as Carrie leaned forward. "Jason loves you. I've never seen him like this before and I am begging you to give him another chance. Whatever he did or said, please try to forgive him."

"He hasn't done anything wrong," Lucy said.

Carrie smiled briefly. "Well, I'm not sure if I believe that entirely. He's my brother and I know better than anyone that he isn't perfect. But he is a good man, and he will spend the rest of his life trying to make you happy if you give him that chance. Will you think about what I said?"

Lucy nodded and Carrie wiped her eyes again before standing. "Good. I'd better go. I'm sorry for disrupting you at work but I didn't know where you lived now."

She walked to the door and paused when Lucy said, "Carrie? Thank you."

"You're welcome," Carrie said. "I hope it works out for you and Jason. I really do."

JASON SLAMMED THE FRONT DOOR BEHIND HIM AND DROPPED his laptop bag in the chair. He rubbed wearily at the back of his neck before turning on the lamp. God, he hated coming home to a dark house. Lucy had lived with him for only a few months, but he had grown used to it scarily quick.

He glanced at his watch. It was close to seven. He had

been out of the office all afternoon for meetings and then stopped at a bar on the way home. He was sorely tempted to sit and drink the rest of the fucking night away but made himself stop after one whiskey. Drinking might numb the pain of losing Lucy for a little while, but it was one hell of a bad idea. He thought briefly of making some dinner and decided against it. His appetite had gone to hell since Lucy left, and most of the dinners his mother had been making and sneaking into his fridge while he was at work had gone straight to the garbage. Who the hell could eat when he had lost the love of his life?

He cocked his head. Lenny, normally so quick to weave around his feet, was nowhere to be seen. A breeze ruffled his hair, bringing with it the scent of the sea. He cursed loudly when he realized the patio door was open a crack. He had gone surfing this morning before work, although even that had lost most of its appeal, and he was certain he had shut and locked the door when he returned.

Panic fluttered in his veins. Since the day Lenny had wandered into his house, skinny, sick, and covered in fleas, he had become a strictly indoors cat but that didn't mean he didn't try to make a break for freedom occasionally. Lucy used to take him outside to the patio with her and cuddle him on her lap, but they never left him alone outside. His heart clenched painfully at the thought of losing Lenny as well.

He ran to the patio door, yanked it open, and stepped out onto the deck. "Lenny! Here kitty, kitty! C'mon Lenny, here kitty -"

The voice died in his throat and hope surged through him when he saw Lucy sitting on the futon. A blanket was wrapped around her legs and Lenny, purring loudly and bumping his face against hers, was sitting with her.

The hope died as quickly as it was born, and he stared silently at her.

She smiled tentatively. "Hi, Jason."

"Here to pick up the rest of your things?"

She shook her head. "No. Will you sit with me?"

He sat down, keeping a safe distance between them. If any part of him touched her, he wasn't sure he could stop himself from just picking her up and carrying her to the bedroom.

"How was your day?" she said.

"Busy. Yours?"

"Terrible, just like every other day for the last two weeks."

"Why are you here, Lucy?"

"To try to explain why I did what I did, to ask for your forgiveness, and to ask you to take me back," she said.

"Yes," he said. He didn't care how pathetic he sounded, living without Lucy was killing him.

Tears shimmered in her eyes and he slid across the futon and put his arm around her. He kissed her, his heart thudding painfully in his chest as she returned his kiss before resting her head on his shoulder.

"I'm so sorry, Jason. More sorry than I can ever say. I was such a – a goddamn idiot and I'll spend the rest of my life trying to make it up to you."

"You don't have to." He buried his face in her hair and breathed deeply. "I love you."

"I love you too and I'm sorry for hurting you, for putting you through hell the last two weeks," she said.

"Come to bed, Lucy," he said. He was desperate to hold her in his arms, to sink deep within her body, and hear her moan his name.

"Jason, just wait, okay?" she said. "I want to try to explain."

"I don't care," he said. "I don't care why you did it, I just want to be with you."

"I want to be with you too, but you deserve an explanation. I need to do this, okay?"

"Okay."

She took a deep breath and stroked Lenny's head. The cat stared adoringly at her as his purring loudened.

"Lenny's missed you," Jason said.

"I've missed him too." She smiled even though the tears were starting to fall.

"Don't cry, little Lucy. Please," he said before wiping them away.

"I've cried so much you'd think I wouldn't have any tears left," she said.

"You and me both."

She bit at her bottom lip. "God, I've really fucked this up. Amanda called me an idiot last night before she slapped me."

"She slapped you?" His arm tightened around her.

She smiled faintly. "It was an intervention. She gave me cookies afterward. She was right, you know. I am a complete and utter moron."

"You're not," he said. "You were just upset and scared."

"Yeah, I was. But that isn't an excuse for what I did." She sighed again. "Jason, I ran because I was – I *am* – terrified that in a few years you'll realize that having kids is more important than you think, and you'll leave me. The thought of losing you terrifies me and that in itself terrifies me. To know that I'm so wrapped up in you, so in love with you that even the possibility of losing makes me feel like I can't breathe, like I'm going to die…"

She trailed off before giving him a grim look. "I am absolutely addicted to you and that can't be healthy. Can it?"

He shrugged. "I don't know. All I know is that I'm just as addicted to you. I won't leave you, Lucy. I love kids and yeah, I want them, but I want a life with you more. If that means never being a dad, then so be it. You are the most important thing in my life, and I can't live without you."

"I can't live without you either." She stared at the ocean. "We're kind of fucked up, Jason Young."

"Maybe," he said. "But if being fucked up means being happier than I've ever been in my life, I can accept it."

She smiled. "Me too."

"Lucy, look at me, honey."

She turned her face toward him. He cupped her cheek before pressing a light kiss on her mouth. "I will never leave you. Not now, not five years from now, not twenty-five years from now. You're stuck with me, Lucy Reid. Whether you like it or not."

"I like it," she whispered against his mouth. "I'm sorry, Jason. Will you forgive me?"

"Yes," he said before kissing her again. "Of course, I will."

"Thank you." She leaned against him and he waited until the tears had stopped leaking down her face before easing away from her. He slipped to one knee on the deck in front of her. She gasped when he pulled the small velvet box from the inside pocket of his jacket and opened it.

She stared wide-eyed at the ring and Lenny made a disgruntled meow when she squeezed him. He clawed at her hands and squirmed free, knocking the ring box from Jason's hand as he jumped to the deck and ran into the house.

"Shit!" Jason grabbed for the box, snagging it just before

it tumbled off the deck to the sand below them. His heart pounding, he held it out to her as she giggled.

"Damn cat," he muttered before wiping a bit of sand from the outside of the box. Luckily, the ring was still firmly wedged in the fabric and he smiled at her as his heart thudded crazily.

"Lucy Reid, will you marry me?"

"Yes, Jason Young," she said softly. "I'll marry you."

Catch up with Jason and Lucy in Elizabeth Kelly's novella, "Breathless". Breathless tells the story of Lucy's best friend Amanda.

Keep reading for an excerpt from "Breathless".

Amanda placed the last of the leftover food in the fridge in Lucy and Jason's kitchen before wiping down the counter and throwing some trash in the garbage. It was close to one in the morning and the party had finally wound down. She leaned against the counter for a moment. She should have been tired, she had been up with Lucy at six this morning, but it wasn't weariness coursing through her body. It was lust, pure and simple.

Lust for Max. Go find him.

No, she absolutely couldn't do that. She was in love with Jamie and just because they technically weren't dating, just because it was months since she'd been laid, didn't mean she could fuck someone else. Besides, she was pretty sure she had seen Max leaving as she was carrying the leftovers up to the house.

She pressed a shaking hand on her lower abdomen and willed her damn pussy to behave itself. She was lucky Max had left. The way she was feeling right now, she'd climb him like a damn tree if she saw him.

She heard footsteps behind her and froze when Max's

deep voice said, "One more dish of leftovers. Is there room in the fridge?"

Her heart racing, she turned and watched as he opened the fridge and shuffled a few things around before placing the dish in the fridge with the others. He shut the door and she clenched her hands into fists when, instead of leaving, he dropped into a kitchen chair and smiled at her.

"Some party, huh?"

She drifted closer to him, she couldn't help herself, and he gave her a puzzled look.

"Amanda, are you okay? You look flushed."

"Max," she whispered, "I…"

She licked her lips and studied his broad shoulders and chest as she stopped in front of him. "I really want to kiss you."

If he was surprised, it didn't show on his face. "Go ahead, Butterfly," he said in that low voice that drove her insane with desire.

She stepped between his spread legs and touched his beard with trembling fingers.

"Don't move," she whispered.

He was so tall that even sitting they were face-to-face. She ran her thumb over his bottom lip before pressing her mouth against his. His lips were warm and firm, and she nibbled at his upper lip before slicking her tongue across the bottom one. He groaned and she probed at the seam of his lips with her tongue. He opened them and she slid her tongue into his mouth. He tasted like scotch and she moaned when he sucked on her tongue before pushing his tongue into her mouth. He touched her crooked tooth with the tip of it then flicked his tongue against hers.

He was unbelievably gentle, and she couldn't get enough of his kisses or of the taste of his mouth. She pressed herself against him and he cupped her ass with those big hands of his and squeezed.

"No moving," she reminded him.

He squeezed her ass again. "This is me not moving. If I were moving, you'd be bent over this table with your dress around your waist and I'd be balls-deep in that hot pussy of yours."

Her mouth dropped open as a tremor of lust, so strong it made her legs shake, swept through her. What the hell was going on? Max was one of the good guys and good guys definitely didn't talk like that.

"That was...unexpected," she said.

He grinned at her. "Was it?"

"Yes, you're a nice guy, Max."

"I am," he replied.

"Nice guys aren't dirty talkers."

He laughed. "How many nice guys have you dated?"

"Not very many," she admitted.

"Let me guess," he licked her throat with his wet tongue, "you like the bad boys. The ones who charm you, fuck you all night, and are gone before you wake up in the morning."

"I didn't say I had good taste," she said as he nuzzled the base of her throat.

"I'm a nice guy," he said. "I don't play games with a woman and if I'm interested in you," he licked her mouth, "there won't be any doubt. And I'll definitely still be in your bed in the morning."

"Because you're a nice guy," she moaned as he nipped at her earlobe.

"Yes," he breathed into her ear, "and because I love waking a woman up with my tongue in her pussy."

"Fuck!" The word exploded from her mouth and he pressed a soft kiss below her ear.

"That too," he said. "Have any of those bad boys you like so much ever woken you up by sucking on your clit, Butterfly?"

She shook her head, her pelvis aching and her nipples throbbing almost painfully, and he squeezed her ass. "You should consider giving us nice guys a chance. Would you like to know why?"

"Yes," she whispered.

He brushed his mouth against hers, just a gentle caress but it made her entire body tingle. He pulled his head back when she tried to deepen the kiss.

"Because the only thing we care about in bed is making sure our woman is completely satisfied. Nothing else matters."

She wanted to tell him that the bad boys did that too but, truthfully, they didn't. At least it wasn't her experience. She told herself numerous times that it didn't matter, she was self-aware enough to know that what she craved was the actual chase. It was all about the excitement of 'will he call or won't he', and the delicious thrill that someone like that would want her, not what the actual sex would be like. When they finally did sleep together, more often than not she was left aching and not fully satisfied.

"Invite me into your bed, Butterfly, and you can ride my dick for as long as you need. You can tie me to your bed and have your dirty way with me if that's what you want," he said with a naughty grin.

She thought of the restraints tucked under the top mattress of her bed. A previous lover had given the 'under the bed restraint kit' to her as a birthday gift, although it had techni-cally been for him not her. She hadn't minded being restrained but it wasn't one of her kinks. She had done it more for his pleasure than hers, but he had refused to allow her to use it on him the one time she had suggested it.

An image of Max, his large body stretched out on her bed with the cuffs around his wrists, flooded through her and her pelvis bucked against him uncontrollably. Jesus, the thought of having control over Max like that was setting her on fire with lust.

"Feels like my Butterfly likes that idea," he whispered before capturing her mouth with his.

This time his kiss was hard and insistent. His previous gentleness was gone, and she returned his kisses eagerly, cupping his face and tracing her fingers over his beard as their tongues battled for control.

"Carrie texted me. She dropped Lucy and Jason at the hotel and she's going to take them to the airport in the morning."

Amanda tore away from Max at the sound of Rita's voice, crossing her arms over her chest and giving Jason's parents a nervous smile as they walked into the kitchen.

"Oh!" Rita said. "Oh, I'm so sorry,"

Her face bright red, Amanda shook her head. "No, I…"

She gave both Jason's parents and Max an apologetic look. "I'm sorry. It's very late and I really should get home. I – I'm sorry," she mumbled again before pushing past Jason's dad and escaping the kitchen.

ABOUT THE AUTHOR

Elizabeth Kelly was born and raised in Ontario, Canada. She moved west as a teenager and now lives in Alberta with her husband and a menagerie of pets. She firmly believes that a person can survive solely on sushi and coffee, and only her husband's mad cooking skills prevents her from proving that theory.

For more information about Elizabeth, check out her website at

www.elizabethkelly.ca

facebook.com/EKellyBooks
twitter.com/ElizabethKBooks
instagram.com/elizabethkelly_author
amazon.com/Elizabeth-Kelly/e/B00EOHZ0MS
bookbub.com/authors/elizabeth-kelly

ALSO BY ELIZABETH KELLY

Tempted Series

Tempted

Twice Tempted

Forever Tempted

Breathless

Tempted Trilogy (Books 1-3)

Red Moon Series

Red Moon

Red Moon Rising

Dark Moon

Alpha Moon

Pale Moon

The Recruit Series

The Recruit (Book One)

The Recruit (Book Two)

The Recruit (Book Three)

The Recruit (Book Four)

The Recruit (Book Five)

The Shifters Series

Willow and the Wolf (Book One)

Ava and the Bear (Book Two)

Broken

An Unlikely Seduction

Holiday Romance

The Christmas Wife

The Christmas Rescue

The Christmas Nanny

The Christmas Boss

Sordid Games